The Dogs of War

Powell glanced out the driver's window of the car and laughed. "There's someone who's making sure he gets his fair share of the spoils," he said, pointing in the direction of a bombed-out storefront.

The young woman journalist sitting beside him in the front seat leaned forward. She saw what Powell was referring to and gasped.

A dog was running through the pedestrian traffic with an arm in its teeth. Severed below the elbow, the forearm and hand trailed a ragged strip of skin, tendons and torn muscle. The fingers still bore rings, and the nails were brightly polished.

"Take a picture," Powell urged her. She turned away. Powell leaned across the seat and grabbed her Nikon. "Come on, take one! That'll look great on the front page. Beirut Goes to the Dogs—Piece by Piece!"

Mack Bolan's
ABLE TEAM

ABLE TEAM
They Came to Kill

Dick Stivers

A GOLD EAGLE BOOK FROM
WORLDWIDE

TORONTO • NEW YORK • LONDON • PARIS
AMSTERDAM • STOCKHOLM • HAMBURG
ATHENS • MILAN • TOKYO • SYDNEY

First edition December 1984

ISBN 0-373-61215-X

Special thanks and acknowledgment to
G. H. Frost for his contributions to this work.

Printed in Canada

1

In the bell tower of the artillery-shattered Greek Orthodox church, Colonel Viktor Dastgerdi put his eyes to the fifty-power lenses of the tripod-mounted siege binoculars. He spun the pan crank to scan the Bekaa Valley and the mountains of eastern Lebanon. Swirling snow blurred the images of rocks and abandoned fields and ice. He panned the optics across the landscape to the gray foothills of the Sahel Mountains. He found the red X.

Ten kilometers away, more than five kilometers into Syria, the X of brilliant-red plastic—two crossed sheets a hundred meters long, ten meters wide—marked the position of a miniaturized transmitter.

Through the binoculars, Dastgerdi saw the red sheets shimmer as gusts of wind tore at the plastic. Storm clouds passed, the late-afternoon light coming in intermittent moments of sudden glare. Sunlight flashed from rocks white with snow. He turned the tripod's altitude crank to drop the aspect of the binoculars and surveyed the narrow, rutted track leading to the target. He saw the truck racing back to the base.

"They are away!" Dastgerdi shouted down to the technicians. "Confirm the signal."

The church had taken several high-explosive shells

during the wars fought in the Bekaa. Only the bell tower and the walls remained, the stones and plaster pitted by shrapnel, the roof timbers and pews carried away by the Iranian Revolutionary Guards for their fires. Syrian technicians manned electronic consoles in the small rooms of the bombed-out sanctuary. Canvas tenting provided shelter from the falling snow.

A radio specialist flipped an audio switch. An oscillating tone came from a monitor. The technician called out to his commander, "Receiving the signal."

"Fire the rockets."

A voice shouted orders, first in Arabic, then Farsi. Below the bell tower, in what had been the main street of the village before the wars came to the Bekaa, Syrians and Iranians hurried away from a truck-mounted 240mm rocket launcher. An officer paced around the rack of Soviet artillery rockets to check the cables and propellant-igniter leads. Then he retreated to the safety of a doorway. Elsewhere in the ruined village—now serving as a base for the Islamic fighters assigned to Dastgerdi—soldiers stood at windows and doorways to watch the launch.

Dastgerdi gave the rocket guidance cones a last glance. The finned cones mounted on the warheads of the rockets represented two years of research and development. Standard-issue Soviet 240mm rockets employed no guidance mechanisms. Launcher crews aimed and fired the rockets like artillery. The rockets being tested today employed microcircuitry to guide them to their targets via small maneuvering fins. Unlike guided missiles, which incorporated complex and expensive computers to find and track their targets, these rockets were guided by the signal generated by a transmitter positioned at the target. The cones on the warheads contained the simple electronic and mechanical parts to modify the trajectory of the falling rockets.

Two years of my life, Dastgerdi thought. But with those rockets, I will kill their President. Then comes the war....

Dastgerdi heard the sound of boots running up the steps. Ali Akbar Rouhani, leader of the Revolutionary Guards stationed at the village, stomped up to the observation post. He stepped past Dastgerdi and put his eyes to the binoculars. When he did not see the target, he grabbed the body tubes and attempted to shift the view. But the binoculars did not move. Rouhani used his strength against the delicate gears of the altitude head.

"This American trash!" Rouhani cursed. "Why does it not operate?"

Dastgerdi spun the cranks, allowing the binoculars to move. Rouhani found the target.

"There!" Rouhani stared for a moment. Then he stepped to an opening in the bell tower's wall and shouted down. "Fire the rockets! What is the—"

A roar obliterated his voice as a rocket streaked away, the flame brilliant against the black clouds. After a second the solid propellant burned out. Another rocket flashed away, then another and another.

A thundering roar came from the storm-dark sky as the supersonic rockets created a noise like a freight train. The thunder faded as the rockets hurtled into the distance.

The Iranian watched the explosions through the

oversized binoculars. "A hit! Two hits! They all hit! Praise be to Allah!"

Colonel Dastgerdi saw the four white-orange sparks on the hillside ten kilometers away. One cloud of yellow marking smoke puffed into the air, the wind blowing the yellow over the hillsides. He called down to his technicians:

"Is there now a signal?"

"No," a voice answered from the canvas shelter. "No more. It is gone."

"Fire the other rockets."

Four more rockets streaked away. Twenty seconds after the launch, four widely spaced puffs of red smoke appeared on the hillsides.

"They all missed!" Rouhani spun away from the binoculars, his face twisting with rage. Spittle sprayed from his mouth and clung in his beard. His eyebrows, one long band of black above his eyes, twisted into a zigzag. "What went wrong? Who is responsible? Who has failed in his service of Allah? You cannot protect your Syrian friends this time."

"The second flight of rockets had no guidance systems," Colonel Dastgerdi explained. Stepping to the binoculars, he studied the distant hillside. Yellow splashes marked the impacts. Explosions had ripped apart the plastic target. Though not achieving pinpoint accuracy, the guided rockets had scored four hits within the hundred meter diameter of the target. He continued his explanation.

"My technicians fitted identical guidance housings to the warheads, but the units contained no electronics or servomechanisms. The first four rockets proved the value of the guidance units, the other four rockets proved the accuracy not to be only by chance.''

"Are you mocking me?" Rouhani demanded.

Colonel Dastgerdi turned away from the binoculars. He saw the Iranian reaching for the Makarov autopistol he wore in a shoulder holster. "No, I am only explaining. Why don't you announce our success to your men? We are within sight of our victory over the Americans."

"We are? But only four hits? What of the four that missed?"

The Iranian had not understood. The colonel explained again. "Four of the rockets had guidance. Four had nothing. The first four proved that my guidance system worked. Announce the success to your men. Victory will come soon."

His hand on his pistol, Rouhani glared at Colonel Dastgerdi for another moment. Then he rushed to the bell-tower window and shouted out, "In the name of Allah, the Compassionate, the Merciful, King of Judgment Day! Allah's promise is true, the hour of doom shall come for the unbelievers! The Americans shall learn of the wrath of Allah...."

Leaving the fanatic to rave, Dastgerdi went down the bell-tower stairs. His Syrian technicians greeted him with salutes and congratulations. Nodding, he stepped into the snow and mud of the street.

Rouhani continued ranting from the bell tower. "I say to the unbelievers, fear Allah! The catastrophe of the Hour of Doom shall be terrible indeed!"

The Iranians answered their leader's pronouncements with slogans. "Death to America the Satan!"

"The evil of their deeds condemns the unbelievers to the scourge of fire!"

"The fire of hell!"

Wind came from the east as a storm came down on the village. Colonel Dastgerdi put up the collar of his greatcoat. Made of fine Soviet wool, identical to the coats of Soviet officers except he had replaced the red stars of the Communist empire with the green Islamic stars of Syria, the boot-length coat kept him warm in any weather.

But soon he would pack his suitcase with the polyester slacks and *quayaberas* popular in Nicaragua.

"Our weapons shall rain fire from the sky!" Rouhani shouted. "The unbelievers will find no shelter from their doom. On that day the earth will be changed into a new earth and the heavens into new heavens, mankind shall stand before Allah, the One, the Almighty. On that day you shall see the guilty in chains, their garments black with filth, and their heads in flames—"

"The wrath of Allah!" the crowd shouted.

"This is a warning to the unbelievers! Our weapons shall fall from the heavens, our weapons shall be the rain of doom. Let the unbelievers take heed, the hour of doom comes!"

Americans and Iranians, two nations of fools! Colonel Dastgerdi laughed out loud as he strode through the falling snow. The American fools, desperate for profits, sold high-technology to their enemies. From electronic components manufactured in California, Dastgerdi had fabricated the rocket guidance system he tested today.

And the Iranians! Crazed with fanaticism and

death wish, led by degenerates like Khomeini and Rouhani, they attacked the decadent and doubt-paralyzed United States at every opportunity, seizing diplomats, bombing embassies, murdering hundreds of U.S. Marines. When the Americans did not respond with devastating counterstrikes, the Iranians declared yet another victory over the Great Satan.

But even the Americans would not allow the murder of their President to pass without revenge.

Dastgerdi knew the future. After the assassination of the President of the United States by Iranian rockets, the rush of events would condemn Iran to destruction and the Middle East to chaos.

And the Soviet empire would capture one more nation.

2

Sitting low in the back seat of the armored Mercedes, Powell waited for the mosque to empty. He held his Galil SAR ready in his hands, a round in the chamber, his thumb on the safety.

Rain drummed on the Mercedes. Powell watched the street, his eyes always moving, searching the doorways and shadows for sudden movement. A hundred meters away, where the street ended at a boulevard, the kerosene lanterns of a café threw yellow light into the darkness. American rock 'n' roll came from the café's jukebox. Two teenage militiamen stood in the café's entry, joking and laughing, their Kalashnikov rifles in their hands. On the rain-glistening asphalt, the long shadows of the militiamen twisted and jumped as the teenagers shifted on their feet, unconsciously moving to the rhythm of the American music.

Of the shops on the street, only the café remained open. The others had closed for the evening prayers. From time to time, Powell scanned the upper floors of the buildings. On one side of the street, firelight flickered in the apartments as women cooked. But on the other side, above the second floor, he saw nothing. Israeli air strikes and Phalangist artillery had shattered the apartments and workshops of the upper floors, leaving only broken concrete.

An old woman with an umbrella and a shopping bag came around the corner. Struggling with the weight of the bag's contents, she carried the parcel for a few steps at a time, then rested, then walked a few more steps. The militiamen stopped joking. They watched the old woman. One teenager ran through the rain to the woman. She turned and started at the sight of the armed man rushing at her.

The teenager greeted her in Arabic. With his right hand draped over his Kalashnikov to steady the rifle, he took the shopping bag with his left. She released the bag and staggered back. The boy spoke quickly to her. His friend's laughter rang out in the narrow street. The old woman pointed her umbrella at a doorway past the Mercedes. The militia teenager accompanied her to her door.

Powell watched them. A young girl opened the door, the oval of her face pale amber in the glow of a flashlight she held. The teenager gave the bag to the girl, then he started back to the café.

As he passed the cars parked in front of the mosque, the teenager glanced inside. He looked into the Mercedes and saw Powell slouched in the back seat. Taking a flashlight from his military web gear, the teenager shone the light inside.

Like the teenager, Powell wore the fatigues and equipment of the Shia Amal militia. His beard and shaggy hair covered his narrow Texan features. Taking his hand off the grip of his Galil, Powell tapped the window where he had taped up a photo of Imam Moussa al Sadr, the spiritual leader of the Shias.

The teenager nodded and returned to his post at the café.

Men came from the mosque. Some crossed the street to their shops and apartments. Others went to the cars. Akbar and Hussain—Powell's Shia operatives—returned to the Mercedes. Hussain strapped on his pistol belt before getting into the car.

"Ready to go," Akbar said in his idiomatic Californian English.

"Don't sweat it," Powell told him. He checked his watch. "We got time."

As Akbar drove through the devastation of West Beirut, he turned to his American friend. "Why don't you come in for prayers?"

Powell answered in Arabic. "The mosque? It would be disrespectful."

"To pray?" Akbar also switched to Arabic. "To seek the mercy and guidance of God is not disrespectful."

Powell paraphrased a verse from the Koran; "Leave me in my error until death overtakes me."

Laughing, Akbar returned to American slang. "But you're no pig-eating Christian dog. You're a righteous dude. I want to save your soul. I want you in the family. But if I don't convert you, I can't set you up with my sister. My old man'd have a shit-fit."

"What mercy would my prayers bring?" Powell continued in Arabic. "Would the prayers of a foreigner stop the killing and the suffering? Could I find understanding of all the horror in prayers?"

"Texan, you're cool, you understand," Akbar jived. But sadness touched his voice for a moment. "You're on our side, so you know."

"I'm not on your side," Powell told the Shia in English. "I'm on my side."

Hussain interrupted with a quotation, "He who fights for Allah's cause fights for himself—"

Powell finished the quote with the next line of Arabic verse. "Allah does not need His creatures' help."

The walkie-talkie buzzed. The voice of Powell's superior came from the tiny speaker. "Calling car three. Report."

Without speaking, Powell clicked the transmit key twice. "That Clayton is so stupid—let's quit the religious talk. We got work to do."

"Yeah, man," Akbar agreed. "Noble deeds."

"A noble deed would be to retire Clayton. That jerk gives the Agency a bad name. Calling for car three! That could get us wasted."

The walkie-talkie buzzed again. "Car three! Report!"

Akbar turned on the citizens-band radio mounted under the dash. Spinning the knob to a channel, he spoke quickly in Arabic, French and English code words. He got a quick answer. "They're parked where they said they would be. I guess the Libyans haven't shown yet."

"Drive up so I can talk to that shit."

After another block, Akbar left the boulevard for a side street. Shattered concrete littered the street. A falling building had crushed a truck. Akbar guided the Mercedes past a line of burned-out cars. He turned two corners. Flashing his high beams twice, he stopped beside a parked panel truck. Powell rolled down his window as his superior made an angry demand.

"Why didn't you answer?"

"Because I want to live! Don't you think there are other radios in the city with our frequency?"

"There's no problem, Powell. We change the frequencies every few days."

"You absolutely positive no one's got our frequency?"

"Absolutely." A balding middle-aged man, Ronald Clayton headed a Central Intelligence Agency surveillance unit assigned to watch the terrorist forces operating in Beirut. An informer had brought Clayton information on a meeting between the Iranian Revolutionary Guard and a Libyan diplomat. Tonight they would follow the diplomat to the meeting place and attempt to identify the leader of the Iranian group.

Powell rolled up his window. "He's so stupid. . . ."

"But he's the boss." Akbar eased the Mercedes around the corner and parked on the boulevard. He turned up the CB radio and listened to the voices and static on the channel. When they heard a voice speak in an unintelligible chaos of languages, Akbar started the car.

Clayton's voice came from the walkie-talkie. "Get ready."

Without acknowledging the instructions, Powell nodded to Akbar. They slowly cruised north on the boulevard. Few cars risked the uncertain safety of the latest cease-fire. They saw only two other vehicles on the dark street.

This section of the city had no electricity. No streetlights illuminated the roadway. No traffic signals flashed at the intersections. Buildings stood black against the darkness of the storm-gray night.

In the vacant lots, fires and lanterns lit the tents of

the homeless. Groups of men with rifles gathered under shelters of plastic sheets to warm themselves around oil-drum stoves.

Past the burned-out businesses and tenement buildings, past the gutted, skeletal ruins of hotels, past the Green Line dividing the city, the skyline of East Beirut stood electric against the night. Thousands of lights marked executive suites and apartments. Swirls of neon marked the theatres, nightclubs, billboards for liquor and perfume. But for the dispossessed of West Beirut—Shias, Sunnis, Druze, Christians—the lights of the wealthy Maronite Christians meant nothing. The war had forced the peasants from the poverty of their mountain villages and thrown them into the poverty and devastation of West Beirut. They had always suffered poverty. The Maronite overlords of Lebanon had always flaunted wealth. In a Beirut divided by an arbitrary frontier called the Green Line, the traditions of Lebanon continued.

In the front seat of the Mercedes, the CB radio alerted the three men. Then Clayton spoke through the walkie-talkie. "We saw the limo. And we're moving. Where are you?"

Again, Powell did not acknowledge his officer's question. But he did rave, "He's so stupid! Why did they send him here?"

Hussain watched the rearview mirror. He glanced back to Powell, and said, "The Libyan comes."

Headlights gained on the Mercedes. They stared forward as a pickup truck with militiamen in the back roared past. Two limousines followed an instant later. The convoy continued ahead, then skidded around a corner.

Clayton followed. Accelerating, weaving past the Mercedes, the panel truck gained on the limousines. A second surveillance car, a Fiat, raced to keep up with the truck.

Powell leaned forward to Akbar. "Slow down. Let Clayton take point if he wants to."

The taillights of the panel truck and the Fiat turned. Akbar stayed two blocks back.

Suddenly, autofire and rocket blasts shattered the night. Powell saw flashes of high explosives over the buildings, and flames fuelled by gasoline. Rifles fired hundreds of rounds.

Akbar floored the accelerator. The Mercedes sped past the narrow street. Looking out the side window, Powell saw only one image.

A street of flames.

3

In the walnut-paneled luxury of an office in Washington, D.C., a senior officer of the Central Intelligence Agency discussed the assassination of a field agent in Beirut. He spoke with a State Department officer of corresponding rank. Both men, career civil servants, wore the uniform of the bureaucrat: three-piece suit, tie, gold cuff links. Their uniforms differed only in color. One man's suit was gray, the other's blue. The State Department paper Viking swiveled in his desk chair, considering the information his counterpart in the Agency was relaying to him.

"A standard surveillance operation. Absolutely no expectation of danger—other than the threat of random violence in that awful place, of course. Our man—his name was Clayton—and his assistants maintained strict procedural discipline. No one outside of the field unit knew of the assignment. Let me emphasize that—no one. If there was a breach of security, it came from someone within the group."

The State Department mandarin interrupted with a question. "Is there any chance your man simply drove into a firefight between rival militias? That he was an innocent bystander, in a sense?"

"Clayton had a good many years of experience in

his work and he wouldn't have blundered into some crossfire between two ragtag gangs. The initial report indicates a carefully plotted ambush. The two cars received intense automatic-weapons fire and several hits from rocket-propelled grenades.''

"Any indication of who supplied the weapons?"

"What?"

"The machine guns, the rockets. Who sponsored this? The Soviets? The Syrians? Or—perhaps this is an utterly Machiavellian thought—is it possible our Israeli friends decided to bloody our nose? With the intent of course of putting responsibility and therefore the blame on the Soviets and their allies?"

"We haven't had a chance to analyze the intent."

"When will you have the evidence from the scene? The forensic evidence?"

"We may never have that evidence. We simply do not have the manpower to send an investigative unit. And I don't know if the spent casings and bullets and whatever other evidence we could find would help us. Every weapon from every nation in the world shows up in Beirut. I think this situation requires interrogation of the personnel involved. To be exact, the Marine who survived."

"A Marine? Does the Agency employ servicemen now?"

"A Marine Corps captain. At least he was. He's now on detached duty with us. He served in the Multinational Peacekeeping Force. Before his Beirut duty, he'd studied Arabic. He became indispensible for our contacts with the fundamentalist Muslim groups, the various Shia gangs."

"What is his ethnic background?"

"Texas."

"Would I know his family? Are they prominent in society?"

The Agency officer laughed. "I doubt it! He's just a shack-town kid who made good in the Marine Corps."

"He's a negro? Is that why he relates to those Mohammedans?"

"No, he's white—"

"Strange."

"He had two years of college on his own before he enlisted. Then he worked hard and scored well on all tests and finally got into officer's training school through the backdoor. Learned passable Arabic somehow. And French. He proved himself in a difficult situation we had in California. Then he volunteered for the Beirut duty. He proved to be a remarkably effective liaison officer."

"How did he survive the attack?"

"He was in the third car. Clayton and the others were in the first and second. Powell saw the ambush and simply drove away."

"Leaving the others to die?"

"Exactly. When he returns to Washington, we'll question him very closely."

"What do you know about his links to Muslim gangs?"

"I know that he's our best man in Beirut, so far as the Shits go—as I call the Shiites. In fact, dismissing him will cost you the single most productive source of street-level information the State Department has in West Beirut. He knows every fundamentalist chieftain and every officer on the staffs of the raghead militias, which proved invaluable during the stationing of the Marine Beirut Force—"

"But which is of negligible value now." The State Department officer looked at his watch. "We really don't want anything to do with those groups. Not on a diplomatic level. For counterterrorism, yes. But his reports don't focus on that, if my memory is correct."

"No, his reports certainly don't. He almost seems to be pleading their case sometimes. Telling us of neocolonialist privileges and discrimination and institutionalized inequality—"

"As if we don't know the realities of demographics and politics there. Should we continue this over lunch?"

"Why? Until we've interrogated him, we'll know nothing more."

"A very unfortunate turn of events."

"True. Mr. Clayton had a promising future with the Agency. We'll miss the loss of his talents. But we will not miss the questionable talents—and the lectures on democracy—of Captain Powell."

4

Powell emptied the drawers of his desk into a cardboard box. The pens, the .45 ACP cartridges, the jagged crescent of shrapnel, the bundle of paperback Korans—all the tools and mementos of his short and difficult career with the Central Intelligence Agency went into a box with Arabic scrawl and the picture of a peach.

Outside the Plexiglas windows of the Agency's East Beirut annex, 155mm artillery shells screamed through the gray morning. Explosions came from the port. Seconds later, the booms of the guns firing came from the Shuf Mountains above Beirut. Both the Phalangists and the Lebanese army had headquarters at the port. Powell went to the window of the west-facing office and tried to look to the northwest. But he couldn't see the target of the shelling.

"Your friends are murdering Christians again," Fisher said from the door. A blond pink-faced man of forty, Fisher had relayed the cable from Washington. "Guess it's a going-away bang for you."

"I don't have any friends with cannons."

"So you say. Here's your ticket to Washington." Fisher dropped an El Al folder in Powell's box of belongings. "Tell it to them."

Powell handed it back to him. "I'll book my own flight. Cancel this one."

"You're going out through Cyprus?"

"I don't know. Maybe they'll open the airport. I'm in no rush."

"Washington wants to debrief you immediately. Repeat, immediately."

"But I don't work for the Agency anymore. If I understand that cable correctly, I'm on my own time now."

"You're out of Beirut, that's what it means. As to your reassignment to another station, Langley didn't cable that information."

"Don't dodge it. I'm out. So I can leave when and how I want. And if I want."

"You want to stay on?" asked an incredulous Fisher.

Powell shrugged. He checked through the drawers a last time. Fisher glanced at the box of objects and books. Seeing the Korans, he started away. "Don't leave just yet," he said. "There's a detail I need confirmed."

"What?"

"Checking a translation." Fisher went to his office and returned with a file of reports. "That Libyan. In a lounge he made a comment—"

"Where?"

Fisher ignored the question. "He made a comment in Arabic that one of our people overheard. Our man translated it, but just to be sure, I had him quote in Arabic also. Look at this, what does that mean?"

Scanning the handwritten script, Powell considered it a moment, then asked, "What was the context?"

"There was a news clip on the television of the President. The ragheads made a series of threats—"

"Ragheads?" Powell interrupted. "You mean, Muslims? Or Palestinians? Or Syrians? Iranians? Libyans? Maybe Aunt Jemima? Who exactly is a raghead?"

"Muslims, whoever, they're all the same. One of them said, 'If the infidel offends thee, strike down the infidel with a sword.'"

"Talk's cheap."

"And the Libyan said, 'The sword rises.'"

"What else?"

"Then the Libyan left for his appointment. You know the rest."

"He said that just before Clayton got wasted?"

"Only minutes before the ambush. Is that quote translated correctly?"

Powell nodded. "The sword rises."

AKBAR AND HUSSAIN led Powell up flight after flight of steel stairs. Artillery and rocket-propelled grenades had punched holes through the reinforced concrete of the stairwell walls. Though workers had cleaned away the debris and repaired the damage the high-explosive and armor-piercing warheads had inflicted on the steel stairs, the gaping holes in the walls remained—some only a hand's width wide, others a meter in diameter. Winter wind and freezing rain came through the holes.

At one landing, Powell found himself staring into storm clouds where an entire section of wall was gone. The stairs and railings had been rewelded and gaps bridged with scrap steel and pipe. Holding onto the rail, Powell looked straight down to the slums and ruined districts of Beirut.

"This is a new one," Powell said to his friends.

"Quite a view, huh?" Akbar asked. "Think I could open a restaurant? Call it the 'Stairway to Heaven.' Hot night spot. Look out at the lights, all that?"

"What lights?" Hussain asked.

"The lights of the city!" Akbar looked at Hussain with surprise. "You didn't listen to the radio this morning. The government announced the restoration of electricity to West Beirut. In forty-eight hours...."

They laughed. Continuing to the next landing, they stopped at the sandbagged post of two sentries. The teenage guards glanced at the handwritten pass Akbar displayed. The pass had the photos of all three men. But this did not satisfy their suspicions. The guards looked at Powell. They studied his face. They noted the Galil SAR and the American Colt .45 he carried. They looked at the Shia uniform he wore. "Who are you?" they demanded.

Akbar answered. "He's one of us. Does not the pass bear his photo and name? Perhaps you should summon our commander for a verification."

"We will." A teenager swung open the door and called into the corridor.

A group of armed men crowded the door. A tall dapper officer in faded fatigues and a beret stepped forward.

"My friend!" He gave Powell a quick embrace and ushered him into the corridor. The uniformed militiamen made way for the two men.

Sayed Ahamed headed a unit of Amal fighters operating in the area of the International Airport. Not a professional soldier, Ahamed had returned from a college in New York with a degree in urban engineering. However, in the chaos and hatred of the Lebanese civil war, no government office would consider the application of a Muslim. Rather than travel to the Gulf states in search of work, Ahamed stayed to fight for the creation of a modern, nonsectarian Lebanon.

Powell had met him when they worked together as coordinators of the Marine patrols, Powell mapping the routes of the Marine platoons through the Shia neighborhoods, Ahamed arranging the preparations for the patrols. In the days and hours preceding the patrols, Ahamed and his units acted as advance men, scouting the narrow streets, questioning residents, watching for outsiders. This prevented incidents. However, after the American administration ordered the guns of its naval force off the Lebanon coast to fire in support of the Christian forces, the Marines—and any friend of the Marines—lost the goodwill of the Shia people. Families gave shelter to anti-American fundamentalist gunmen. Snipers fired on Marines. Ahamed could no longer send in his men without casualties. The Marines abandoned the patrols due to the extreme risk.

In the months that followed, the Marines became prisoners within their compound, under fire from every extremist sect and gang. The militias fought an endless battle of unreported skirmishes with units of the Palestine Liberation Army, the Islamic Amal splinter group, the Iranians, the Druze and Syrian terror teams, infiltrating with the goal of murdering

Marines. The Syrians and Iranians finally resorted to a truck bomb to penetrate the concentric rings of Christian security, Shia security, then the few Marines with unloaded rifles who manned the gates to the compound. Hundreds of United States Marines died. The two friends—Ahamed from a village in the Shuf Mountains and Powell from a one-drugstore town in Texas—refused to hate each other for the mistakes of fools educated at Harvard and Yale.

"The others are waiting," Ahamed told Powell, his arm around his American friend's shoulders.

"I don't work for the Agency anymore."

"What? They—"

"They fired me."

"They take this killing of Clayton so seriously? Why?"

Powell stopped outside the door to the conference room. He glanced at the guards standing in the corridor of the blasted hotel. They would not hear. Cold wind blew through a shell hole at the far end of the corridor as Powell talked quietly in English to the Shia officer.

"There is something I cannot talk about in there. I need your help. The Libyan that Clayton was following had something to do with an Iranian named Rouhani. Rouhani's with a gang of Revolutionary Guards out in the Bekaa. The Libyan has an organization and millions of dollars to give away and Rouhani wanted in on it. They're planning something and I want to find out what it is."

"Another attack on Americans? Perhaps Europeans?"

"Would I care—" Powell faked shock "—if the

Iranians killed some French or English? I would con-
tribute to the cause of killing pacifists and hypo-
crites. Kill the queen, kill the head of the European
Common Farce, I mean kill them all! Seriously, I
doubt if the Iranians would need the organization or
money to hit a target in Lebanon.''

"Israel?''

"They could get the money from the Syrians or
Palestinians. I think the Iranians want to hit a target
outside of Lebanon, maybe in the United States.''

"But you are no longer with your government.''

"If I break up a gang trying to hit the United
States, maybe I'll get my job back.''

"We cannot allow uncontrolled elements to operate from our country,'' Ahamed said. "You know
I'll give you whatever help you need.''

"Knew you'd say that. Let's go in.''

The leaders of the several Amal militias stationed
in Beirut faced Powell. They did not waste time on
greetings or polite conversation.

"What do the clowns think now?''

"Do they accuse us in the murders?''

"What was the report you sent to Washington?''

"Does this mean more weapons and dollars for the
Fascist warlords?''

Powell waited until all the chieftains had asked a
question, then calmly responded. "It means that
Clayton's dead and you've got one less clown in the
Agency. It also means that I am now a private citizen, persona non grata with the United States government. They don't care what my report said, they
don't care what the truth is.''

"Do they believe it is the work of our people?''

"Of course," Powell answered. "All Shias are terrorists. Don't you read the newspapers?"

"We don't need the United States."

"Yes, you do. And the United States needs your friendship. That is why I will disregard the orders from my superiors. I will not return to the United States until I know who the killers of that dog Clayton are. Because I will not have the support of my government, I am here now to ask for your help."

Sayed Ahamed spoke to the others. "Powell has always told the truth."

"Unlike his despicable President and diplomats," one chieftain declared.

Powell stared past the table where the chieftains sat. The plate-glass windows of the hotel conference room overlooked the gray Mediterranean. Wind-whipped whitecaps flecked the surface.

Again Sayed Ahamed took Powell's side. "He has nothing to do with his President. Will we help him in his search? It was not our people who killed the American agent. It can only be to our benefit if my friend discovers the truth."

The militia chieftains nodded.

5

Lyons guided the rental car through the maze of streets in the industrial park. He circled around parked diesels and inched through groups of workers crowding around catering trucks. Finally he found the address of the workshop.

Parking in a space marked For Clients Only, the tall, square-shouldered ex-LAPD detective took two cases—one long and flat, the other the size of an airline flight bag—from the back seat. He pushed through a plate-glass door to a tiny reception room.

A secretary looked up from a stack of order forms. Almost sixty, with brilliant false teeth and white hair, she glanced to the cases he held and then pressed an intercom button. "They're expecting you, sir."

"If I get a call, can you switch it to a phone in there?" Lyons asked.

"Yes, sir. Certainly."

Lyons started to say something else to the woman when a strong deep voice cut across the room.

"So! You're the one Andrzej always talked about." Lyons turned to see a wiry black man standing in the doorway. He wore a denim shop apron, and his chest pocket had a plastic liner holding pens and pencils and a micrometer. He motioned for

Lyons to enter. "I'm Randall. I'll introduce you to the others."

As if to free his right hand for a handshake, Lyons transferred the flight bag to his left hand. He carried both cases with one hand as he paused in the doorway.

Lyons did not trust anyone associated with the Central Intelligence Agency. Though these technicians had been friends of Andrzej Konzaki, he expected the worst. His eyes scanned the workshop before he entered. His right hand remained free and ready to grab the Colt Python he wore under his sports coat.

Steel cabinets dominated two walls. Machines and workbenches took the other walls. On the opposite wall, an open door revealed a dimly lit corridor. He saw a beer-bellied technician standing up from a drill press. Another man looked up from a workbench covered with tools and the components of a Kalashnikov rifle. Lyons saw no one else.

He finally entered.

The beer belly approached, smiling, his hand out in greeting. "Hi, Carl. I'm Lloyd. Konzaki and I were in the Corps together."

"And I'm Bob," the other technician said. "Andy called me the jeweler. He ever mention me?"

"Yeah, he did." Lyons shook hands with the three men.

"There was some work even Andy couldn't do," Bob said. "I was his specialist. A specialist for the specialists, that's what he called me. In fact, I did some of the work on your Colt Frankenstein."

In four quick strides, Lyons crossed the workshop

and glanced through the open door leading to what he assumed to be a corridor. He saw a fifty-foot-long firing lane with mechanical targets at the far end.

"That's where we test-fire our work," Randall told him. "Saves us driving out to a rifle range."

"So, how can we help you?" Bob asked.

"I need my weapons checked. Maybe they need some work, maybe not. Can't take them to a gunsmith."

"Konzaki's creations!" Bob looked like a kid invited to a party. "They've been out there a year. Let's see how they look. They hold up okay?"

"No problems," Lyons said, snapping open the larger case. "This is preventive maintenance. The Atchisson." He zipped open the flight bag. "Here's the Colt."

Randall picked up the heavy selective-fire assault shotgun. "Why do you call this an Atchisson? It isn't, you know."

"Because that's what Konzaki told me."

With the confidence of expertise and long familiarity, Randall explained the differences. "My man, what you have here is a redesigned and reengineered Armalite rifle incorporating components of other weapon designs. Notice the receiver and the handle and the grip and all that. This is not an Atchisson. Bob, could you please get me a for-real Atchisson while I set this man straight?"

The technician went to a set of the steel cabinets and opened a door to reveal a rack of shotguns. He took three shotguns out. Randall continued his explanation.

"You see, this Konzaki-created wonder weapon

represents the fusion of several designs. Components designed by the immortal Mr. Stoner. Components by Mr. Atchisson. And of course, components designed by Andrzej.''

Bob put the shotguns on the workbench. Randall picked up an odd weapon with two pistol grips. ''Notice the box magazine. Notice the lack of a shoulder stock. This is a fully automatic submachine shotgun made by the Muslim gunsmiths of the Phillipines. Made before 1970. No semiauto. Undependable safety. Metal crystallized and subject to stress cracking. But this may represent the beginning of the modern assault shotgun. The designer didn't take a semiauto shotgun and make it full-auto. The maker redesigned a submachine gun to fire twelve gauge.''

''Open the thing up, professor,'' Bob interrupted. ''Show him the bolt, that's what's different.''

''I was getting to that.'' Randall opened the receiver of the Phillipine shotgun. ''I know all this stuff and nobody wants to listen to the details. Man, frustrating. Look. Here's the bolt. Is that heavy? That's the single most important design change, that heavy bolt. Heavy bolt, then heavy springs, heavy sear mechanism, heavy receiver—got to make it heavy duty to fire 12-gauge.''

Lyons weighed the bolt in his hand. ''That's why my Atchisson's so heavy?''

''You don't have an Atchisson,'' Randall corrected.

''Then what is it?''

''Call it a Konzaki, whatever. Here's the Atchisson.'' Randall picked up the futuristic selective-fire assault shotgun. He touched the components as he identified each one. "Atchisson made this from existing components. Incorporates the front hand guard and stock from an M-16. Thompson pistol grip. Browning trigger mechanism. What's new is the receiver and bolt. This receiver," he said, indicating the long cylindrical housing going from the barrel to the shoulder pad, "houses the world's heaviest bolt, that is, for an assault weapon. Three pounds. Operates on the blowback principle. Pull the trigger, the firing pin pops the round, the recoil drives the bolt back. This bolt goes all the way back in the receiver tube. Since he went into production, Atchisson's making these with a different look, but the mechanism is the same. Now this is an excellent weapon, but Konzaki didn't like the reciprocating bolt handle. If the handle's moving forward and backward with the bolt, things could get jammed into this long slot here. Didn't like that. So he figured he'd use Armalite components to put together his version—"

"Also," Lloyd interrupted, "he wanted the shotgun to look like an M-16. In the Corps, we learned that the man who carried the unusual weapon got hit first. If an enemy sniper had a platoon coming, and he had the chance to pick the target for his first shot, he'd shoot the man who looked like the officer or weapons specialist. So the man carrying the .45 auto would get hit, or the man with the M-60, or a man carrying the fancy subgun. Andy said he didn't want you drawing more than your share of fire, so he made his shotgun look like a standard weapon."

"Yeah, makes sense," Lyons said.

"Damn right," Lloyd emphasized. "We've been there. We know what you're up against."

"Returning to my discussion of this fascinating creation of our late dear friend," Randall resumed, snapping open the selective-fire assault shotgun Konzaki had custom-fabricated for Lyons. "On the outside, it looks like an oversized M-16. But on the inside, it gets radical. Heavy blowback bolt, heavy springs, heavy buffer spring, heavy trigger mechanism. Operating features of an M-16, but the firepower of 12-gauge. How has it worked?"

"It knocks them down. Almost useless past a hundred feet."

"What about with slugs?" Bob asked.

"I shot at a rifleman one time," Lyons told them. "He was about a hundred yards away."

"A hundred yards!" Lloyd marveled. "With shotgun slugs? You positive?"

"Situation got desperate. They had us in a no-exit ambush. He was moving into a position to fire down on us. I put in a magazine of slugs and kept shooting until one hit him. It was hit him or die."

"But the Konzak got you out," Randall said, nodding.

"Konzak," Lyons repeated. "Yeah, that's the name. Konzak Assault Weapon. So can you check this thing out?"

"Sure, no problem." Randall glanced at the Konzak components.

"What we'll do is X-ray it," Bob suggested. "Eyeball it for extreme wear and tear. Then X-ray it to look for crystallization, hairline cracks."

"What about that super-Colt Konzaki put together?" Lloyd asked. "How's it holding up?"

Lyons took the modified-for-silence Colt Government Model out of the flight bag. The gun had been redesigned and hand machined by Andrzej Konzaki to incorporate the innovations of the state-of-the-art Beretta autopistols. The interior mechanisms of the Colt no longer resembled what Browning had invented and patented. But it fired silent, full-powered .45-caliber slugs, in semiauto and 3-shot-burst modes, at a thousand feet per second.

"How many rounds have you fired through it?" Randall asked as he took the pistol from Lyons. After checking the chamber he folded down the left-hand grip lever and sighted on the wall.

Lyons considered the question for a moment, thinking back over the past year, counting the missions and the firefights. "In action, a few hundred. But after every mission I fire a minimum of a hundred rounds through it. I try to break it at the range—"

"Instead of it breaking in the field," Lloyd added. "There it is, break it when you can fix it. What's the accuracy?"

"At combat distance, it's good enough."

"What's that distance?" Lloyd asked.

"Fifty feet or less. Usually arm's distance."

"What about farther than that?"

"I've got the Interdynamics for that."

"Oh, yeah," Lloyd nodded. "That kit that silences an M-16."

"But only one shot at a time," Bob commented.

"The other guys have got Berettas," Lyons told him. "The Berettas are more accurate at a longer distance, even though they don't have any knock-down power. But then neither does the Interdynamics."

Randall flipped the left-hand grip lever up and down. The lever provided a firm hold for the shooter's left hand, converting the pistol to a compact submachine gun. "When Konzaki started working on this thing, I didn't know what that man thought he was doing. But it worked."

"How's it compare to the Berettas?" Bob asked.

"Nine millimeter was designed for killing Europeans," Lyons told him. "For dangerous people, you need a .45."

The technicians laughed at the sardonic comment.

"Okay, okay." Randall gathered up the weapons. "Time to work. Maybe we can swap jokes after working hours. When do you need these things back?"

"Soon as possible. Immediately. Don't like being without them."

"Konzaki said you were like that," Randall added, his voice going quiet. "We got to get together and talk about that guy. You know, there wasn't a funeral or wake. Nothing. We just got the word that he was gone. Nothing else. It just seems so unreal that he isn't around anymore."

"That's the way it is. But I don't know what I can tell you about it. I'll have to check with my people about what's classified and what isn't."

"He went out on a mission with you?" Lloyd asked, incredulous. "The guy didn't have any legs."

"The action came to him. That's all I can say." The pager at Lyons's belt buzzed. "Speaking of action, I need a phone."

"There—" Randall pointed to a phone on the workbench. "And that line's secure, by the way."

"Secure from the Agency?" Lyons asked.

"No," Randall told him. "Don't say anything you don't want Langley to know."

Lyons dialed a number and waited, then punched in another series of numbers for the access code. Rosario Blancanales, his Puerto Rican partner on Able Team, answered.

"We've got an assignment," the Politician said. "When can you get back?"

"I'm at the Agency workshop."

"Let's don't talk about that on the telephone—" Blancanales began.

"This phone's secure from the public," Lyons said. "But not from the Agency."

"That's an Agency phone?"

"Just don't say anything about business. Any equipment you want me to pick up while I'm here? Agency-type equipment?"

"We can talk. It's an Agency job. We'll be going to Beirut to pick up one of their people. He's gone over to the Amal militia and the Agency wants him for interrogation here."

"Why don't they do their own dirty work?"

"The people they had are deceased."

"So they want us to go?"

"That's the mission. Pick up and bring back."

"What if their man doesn't want to come back?"

"Bang."

"Like that?"

"Just relaying the instructions. Soon as you get here, we go."

"Give me a few hours. Later." Lyons hung up and

returned to the technician. "Can you do a rush job on the checkouts?"

"You're working?" Randall asked.

"Dirty work for the Agency."

Randall looked to the two other men. "What do you think?"

Bob shrugged. "Service while you wait."

6

Footfalls crunched on broken glass.

Powell lay on his living-room couch and listened as the slow, careful footsteps—advancing, pausing, advancing again—approached his apartment door.

Throughout the night, battles had raged. Militias hammered opponents with mortars and automatic weapons, explosions and firefights tearing up the neighborhoods along the Green Line dividing the city. From emplacements near the port, the Phalangists shelled the Druze in the Shuf Mountains, then Druze and Syrians replied with artillery and rockets.

The accurate 155mm high-explosive shells blasted the Christian forces near the port, but the barrages of Soviet 120mm and 240mm rockets fell throughout the city, indiscriminately killing and maiming Christians and Muslims.

One rocket hit a neighboring apartment house. Powell woke to screams and sirens. He left his bed and went to sleep on the couch. His bedroom opened to the balcony and a view of the mountains, but the living room had no windows, only a door to the hallway. The extra wall of masonry between him and the explosions would stop glass and shrapnel if a rocket hit his balcony.

Before dawn, the fighting stopped. Quiet returned

as the sirens of ambulances taking the wounded to hospitals faded. The city remained unnaturally quiet, without the sounds of the morning traffic rush, as commuters and truck drivers waited in the uncertain safety of their homes rather than risk driving into another barrage of high explosives and phosphorus.

In the strange quiet, Powell listened for sounds outside his apartment door, and heard footsteps.

He thumbed off the safety on his Colt. Listening, he visualized the hallway. The explosion in the next apartment building had shattered the windows at the end of the hall, spraying broken glass over the linoleum.

Assassins did not come alone. They worked in teams. Unless they intended to bomb him. A killer? Phalangist? Iranian? Islamic Amal? Libyan? The thought of who might have paid an assassin to kill him distracted him for a moment as his memory reviewed the long list of his enemies. He gave up the effort.

Who cares who it is? They came to kill.

Slipping from under his blanket, Powell went silently into the bedroom. He put on sneakers, then his Kevlar vest. Through the dirty glass and blurry anti-shatter plastic film of the sliding balcony doors, he scanned the opposite rooftops. He saw nothing unusual, no one waiting to shoot as he came out. He slid the door open and stepped into the freezing morning.

He crossed his balcony to the balcony of the next apartment. The family living there had moved from the apartment after a hit from an RPG killed their infant boy and the grandmother. Since then, Powell had paid the rent on the apartment. He glanced through the shattered windows, saw no one in the empty interior. He hurried over the dust and blood-stiff carpets to the hallway door.

Months before, he had installed three fish-eye peepholes in this door. One lens looked to the right, one to the center, the third to the left. The three peepholes gave him a view of the entire hallway.

He saw a pale young man in heavy coat and wool hat knocking on his door. No one else.

By touch, Powell keyed the combination of the padlock on the heavy steel bar securing the door. He threw open the door and extended the pistol, sighting on the head of the wool-capped figure.

The figure turned, mouth opening, eyes going wide. Powell was almost as surprised. The person at the other end of the barrel was a woman! Stumbling backward, she almost fell, but braced herself against the wall. "Don't—don't—please don't shoot. I—"

"Who are you?" Powell demanded.

"I'm here to see—" She recovered from her shock and studied him for a moment. "I'm here to talk to you."

"Then answer me! Who are you?"

"Anne Desmarais, I'm a journalist."

"French?"

"Yes, from Quebec."

"Why you creeping around out here?"

"Creeping? The glass could cut my tennis shoes—and there are no numbers on the doors."

"Isn't that a shame. What do you want?"

"I want to interview you about the killing of George Clayton."

"Clayton who? Don't know who you're talking about. You must have the wrong address." Powell started to shut the door.

"I'll exchange information!" she called out.

"What information?"

"I don't want to talk out here."

"What information?" he insisted.

She stepped closer to him. Her right hand went into her coat pocket. Powell aimed the Colt at her face. She explained quickly, her voice tight. "I have a photo—here. This is the Iranian who had Clayton killed. His name's Rouhani."

The grainy black-and-white print showed two men talking. One had the unkempt hair and beard of the Iranian Revolutionary Guard. The other wore the Soviet-style greatcoat with the insignia of the Syrian army.

"Who's the other one?" Powell asked.

"Want to talk, American?"

"Sure, wait here." Powell closed the door and replaced the steel bar and combination lock. He waited a few seconds, then looked through the peepholes. The woman stood. No one moved at the ends of the hallway. Powell went back to his apartment. He paused to pull on his fatigue pants and shirt. Then he buckled on his black nylon shoulder holster for his Colt autopistol.

He listened for movement in the hallway before throwing open the door and standing aside.

"Who do you think I am?" she asked as she walked into his apartment.

"I don't know." He kicked the door closed and slid the locking bar across. Keeping the cocked and unlocked Colt pointed at the ceiling, he slapped the pockets of her coat with his left hand, finding a change purse, a note pad and pen, several photos, a roll of Lebanese pounds. He threw the note pad and photos on the couch. Returning to the search, he jammed his hand inside her coat to check for weapons and she slapped at him as he touched her breasts.

"Stop it!"

"Then take off the coat! Move wrong and you're dead!"

"The freedom fighters have you Americans shaking," she said as she shrugged off her coat and let it slide to the floor. She wore a snug sweater, jeans and tennis shoes. A Nikon with a zoom lens hung around her neck. Around her waist she wore a web belt with several pouches. By touch, he found her identification, then her film, a flash unit, another lens and various accessories. He threw her Canadian passport and papers on the couch.

"That military gear could get you killed," he told her.

"I'm a journalist. All sides respect my neutrality."

"Dream on, *mademoiselle*." Powell sight-checked her. Her tight jeans concealed nothing. He jammed his fingers in the back of her waistband. He found only the sheer synthetic of her underwear. She recoiled from his touch. Then he patted her armpits, and in the instant before she twisted away, felt the undersides of her breasts.

"Don't touch me like—" she sneered.

"What do you have in your bra?"

"You pig! You Americans—"

"What is it? Take it out!" Powell shouted.

Turning away, she put her hands under her sweater. Powell jerked her around to face him. Defiant, she pulled up her sweater, exposing the white flow of her abdomen, then her bra.

She pulled a disc of foam out of one brassiere cup. The foam had been cut to conceal a microcassette recorder. She passed it to him. He threw it on the couch, then reached into the other side of her bra and pulled out the other pad. It had a few U.S. hundred dollar bills, traveler's checks and a thousand-franc note in a plastic envelope.

"I have never been searched like this before! Never!" she said, her voice shaking with anger.

"You never came here before." He snatched the hat off her head, and her black, lustrous hair fell to her shoulders. He found nothing inside her hat.

"Sit down there," he told her, pointing to a chair across the room. The search over, he took a moment to look at her, enjoying the fine-boned features of her face, the white flow of her throat. He remembered the warmth of her body against his hands and smiled.

She sat in the chair and stared back contemptuously. He sat on the couch several steps away. Setting the safety on his Colt, he placed the gun on the coffee table in front of him. Then he picked up the microcassette recorder. He watched the reels turning for a moment. Grinning to her, he popped out the cassette and put it in his pocket.

"Now you're a thief!" she cried.

Powell laughed. He flipped open her passport. He verified her name and nationality, then read the entry

and exit stamps. In the year since the passport had
been issued, she had traveled first to El Salvador,
then Guatemala, Mexico, the United States, then to
Nicaragua several times, then to France, West Germany, East Germany, Italy, Syria, and finally to
Lebanon. He sailed the passport and papers back to
her.

"You do get around."

"It is my work."

"For what newspaper?"

"I am a free-lance journalist. I came to talk about
Rouhani and the murder of the CIA agent."

"How'd you get that photo?"

"We will exchange information?"

"Depends."

"On what does it depend?"

"What you want to know and what I want to tell
you." He opened up her note pad and leafed through
it. She wrote in French, a precise typewriterlike print-
ing of words and symbols and abbreviated names. He
skimmed her notes, recognizing many of the names
and places. As he read her quotes and observations,
he talked to gain time. "Got your own personal
shorthand. What's it say?"

"Don't you speak or read French? It is the most
important language here! The first language of the
educated people."

"I'm just a Texas kid." He read that Sayed Ahamed had told her he knew nothing of American
operations in Beirut or Lebanon, that he knew
nothing of the ambush of the American agent, but
that he hoped all foreign imperialists suffered the
same fate. Powell continued jiving the Canadian

journalist. "Only French I ever heard was Louisiana Creole. And sometimes that crazy Creole you Cuebek-cuys talk."

"Quebecois!" she pronounced. "Mr. Powell, I didn't come here to do a biographical sketch of the quintessential American intelligence agent. I want to talk to you about the assassination two nights ago of George Clayton, your superior officer."

He looked up from reading her notes. "Who's this? When?"

She ignored his questions. "My sources told me the late Mr. Clayton intended to follow First Secretary Baesho to a meeting with Rouhani and to photograph the other representatives of the peoples' revolutionary forces who attended the meeting. What does the Agency believe went wrong?"

"Look, honey, if I were with the CIA, I couldn't answer those questions, but I'm not, so I don't even know what you're talking about. But that Iranian you talked about, I'm interested in him. Did he have something to do with murdering that American?"

"If you're not with the Agency, why do you care?"

" 'Cause I hate those raghead motherfuckers! I'm AWOL, but I'm still a Marine, and I got one heavy payback to deliver."

"It's a personal crusade, this payback? My sources said you were a Marine. That is, before you joined the Central Intelligence Agency."

"I'm no agent. I tell you, I wouldn't work for those jackoffs, they're just too much stupid."

"You say you're absent without leave from the United States Marine Corps. What are you doing in Beirut?"

"Can't go home, you know. Unless I want to go to prison."

"You're wearing the uniform of the Amal militia. Are you now serving with the Shia forces?"

"Gotta work. No welfare here, not for American Marines on the run. But I don't want to talk about me. I want to know about that there Iranian. Where'd you take that picture? And who's the other dude?"

"There's more photos in my notebook. In the back. They are difficult to find."

Powell flipped open the notebook and folded back the cover. In his hurry to read her notes, he had missed a slit in the vinyl of the notebook. The woman had concealed several photos between the vinyl and the cardboard of the cover.

"There. Look through all the photos. I believe you'll speak with me now. I want the story of the killing. And you want the killers."

Taken from the roof of a building, looking down at the street, the first grainy photo showed a limousine followed by a panel truck. The next photo showed the panel truck and a Fiat in the center of the block. The third photo caught the flashes of rifles and the long flame of a rocket. The next photos showed the explosions and flaming hulks. Powell finally looked up to the young woman.

"Who took these pictures?" he asked.

"I did."

"You were waiting for it to happen?"

"I wasn't told what would happen. I was told to wait and watch. I was told it would be a diplomatic meeting."

"Who told you?"

"You want to meet him?"

"Who is he?"

"He wants to speak with you. He is also an American. He did not know what would happen that night until it occurred. He realizes that the killing of Clayton now jeopardizes his life."

"I asked, who is he?"

"You want to meet him? I'll take you to him."

Powell holstered his Colt. "Let's go," he said.

7

In the front seat of the parked taxi, Carl Lyons
sipped sweet French coffee flavored with nutmeg and
vanilla. He watched the street and the apartment
house while he savored the warm spicy drink. His
eyes were always searching, flicking from the apartment entry to the balconies and rooftops overlooking
the street, then scanning the sidewalks and doorways
before returning to the street door. Sometimes he
glanced at the rearview mirror.

The neighborhood appeared deserted. No cars
moved on the street. Debris from rocket strikes—
glass, concrete, pieces of furniture—littered the
asphalt. Wads of bloody bandages on the sidewalk
marked the site of the tragedies and suffering during
the night.

Lyons glanced at his watch. Six-thirty in the morning. The start of the morning traffic rush. Fifteen
minutes had passed since the young woman arrived in
a taxi and then entered the agent's apartment house.
Five minutes since Lyons poured his third cup of
spiced coffee.

Three hours before, Able Team had flown from
Cyprus via private plane. Now, with cameras and
tape recorders as props for their roles as American
journalists, they waited outside the apartment of the

renegade CIA agent, Lyons and Blancanales watching from the taxi, Gadgets maintaining electronic surveillance from the rooftop.

The taxi driver—Pierre, a Phalangist agent provided by the Agency—slept over the steering wheel, snoring. He shifted in the seat, then opened his eyes and glanced around. He returned to sleep. Blancanales slept in the back seat. He would take the next surveillance shift.

An electronic buzz started the driver awake. Lyons set down his coffee. Gadgets's voice came to them through the encoding circuits of the hand radios Lyons and Blancanales carried.

"He's coming down. That girl's with him."

"You got a mike on them yet?"

"On his car. I'm up on the roof now. I'll go into his apartment while you're following them."

"See you later."

Able Team did not fear the interception of their radio transmissions. Designed and manufactured to the specifications of the National Security Agency, their hand radios employed encoding circuits to scramble every transmission, to decode every message received. Without one of the three radios Able Team carried, a technician scanning the bands would intercept only bursts of electronic noise.

"Hey, Pol, wake up," Lyons said to his partner.

"I'm awake. I'll stay down until we're moving. You see him?"

In the back seat, Blancanales turned on a VHF receiver-recorder unit. The radio received the transmissions from the miniature microphones placed by Gadgets and recorded the monitored conversations.

"No problem," Lyons told him. "We'll watch him for a while. Watch and listen. Got anything yet?"

Blancanales turned up the volume of the monitor. The tiny speaker issued static and the sounds of distant voices and a clanging metal gate. Footsteps echoed in a garage.

"But we cannot take him," Pierre protested. "One way, other way, the girl is a problem. A witness. It would be better if no one knew."

"We have time," Blancanales answered. "The Agency wants information. We'll get some."

"Then we'll get the man," Lyons added.

They heard distinct voices and footsteps. As they listened, car doors opened and closed. Then they heard the voice of the agent.

"...understand, it's not that I don't trust you, *mademoiselle*, it's just that I don't know what to expect. So pardon me if I take a little look-see around his place before we go waltzing in."

"That's your prerogative."

As the car's engine started, as the voices continued, Lyons turned to Blancanales. "I've heard that voice before! This Powell guy, you think—remember that Marine out at Twenty-Nine Palms that time? The captain who spoke all those languages? Reminds me of him."

"There was nothing in the background dossier about that," Blancanales said.

Lyons listened to the agent making conversation with the woman. "Wow, maybe it is. And I thought that Marine was a stand-up fellow."

A battered black Mercedes left the apartment building's underground garage. Pierre waited a few seconds, then started the engine and put the taxi in gear. As he followed the Mercedes, he glanced to the two Americans and said, "Yes, this Powell was a Marine. Before he worked for the CIA. Before he betrayed us and joined the Communists. Very strange, isn't it?"

Lyons and Blancanales exchanged glances. After a moment Lyons finally agreed. "Yeah, strange."

"WHO IS IT we're going to meet?" Powell asked her as they drove through the cold gray streets. "How 'bout breaking down and telling me his name?"

"I will introduce you when you meet."

On the boulevards, they had finally encountered traffic. An hour of quiet had persuaded the citizens of Beirut to brave the streets. Now, bumper-to-bumper lines of Mercedes sedans, Fiats and rusting Cadillacs wove through the rubble of collapsed buildings. Hulks of burned cars and trucks lined streets devastated by shellfire. At an intersection Powell wove his Mercedes through a jam of ambulances, medics and work crews digging through a pile of broken concrete that had been an apartment house.

Powell glanced out his window and laughed. He pointed. "There's someone who's taking their share of the spoils."

"What?" Desmarais asked. She couldn't see what he meant.

"That dog...there!" Powell pointed in front of the car. "Think I could get rich, marketing that brand of dog food? Export Beirut's number-one product."

The young woman leaned forward. Finally she saw, and gasped.

A dog ran through the traffic with an arm in its teeth. Severed below the elbow, the hand and forearm trailed a ragged strip of skin and tendons. The hand still had rings and nail polish.

"Take a picture!" Powell told her. She turned away. Powell leaned across the seat and grabbed her Nikon. "Come on, take one! That'll look great on a front page. 'Beirut Goes to the Dogs, Piece by Piece.'"

A Kalashnikov popped. As Powell idled past, a militiaman kicked the dead dog. He picked up the arm and stripped off the rings, then dropped the arm beside the dog.

"So what do you think of Beirut, Mademoiselle Desmarais?" Powell joked.

"Are you proud, American? Do you not feel even the slightest shame for what your country has done to the Lebanese? The rape of their country, their traditions? You and your Israeli friends?"

"Bitch! Shut up! I read history books. All this started a long time before there was even a U.S. of A. Before Columbus. Before—"

"Oh, you can read?"

Turning onto a side street, Powell slowed for a moment as he buttoned his overcoat to conceal his uniform, then he accelerated. After two more turns, he snaked through an unmanned roadblock of oil drums and sandbags. He stopped at a second roadblock and rolled down his window.

Militiamen in mismatched uniforms and weapons approached the Mercedes. As one watched the interior of the car, another took the plastic-sealed pass Powell offered. Other militiamen—teenagers in jeans and leather coats and stained Lebanese army coats—stood back several steps, casually gripping their Kalashnikov and M-16 rifles.

A Shia officer who knew Powell waved and called out in Arabic. Powell ignored his friend's greeting. Confused, the officer leaned down to look at the face of the bearded, shaggy-haired American.

Powell spoke loudly. "Don't want no problems, Commander. Just taking my girlfriend on a tour of the Casbah."

A militiaman translated for the officer. Understanding, the Shia grinned and nodded. He said in broken English, "Very good, sir. Very good. Have good day. Hello."

Powell accelerated away.

As THE TAXI SLOWED to a stop at the roadblock, Lyons watched the Mercedes disappear around a corner. The voices of Powell and the woman faded as Blancanales turned down the monitor volume and covered the receiver-recorder with a camera-equipment case. Militiamen surrounded the car and looked inside.

"Journalists," the Phalangist driver called out.

The officer pointed at the taxi driver and gave him an order in Arabic. The driver waved his pass. Militiamen jerked open the door and dragged out the driver.

An AK muzzle tapped Lyons's window. A militiaman shouted, "Out! Get out!"

Explosions blasted away the shouts. Militiamen

ran for cover, but the officer and two men still held the driver. American dollars appeared in the taxi driver's hand. Waving the money, he stood up. The officer returned the pass and took the handful of twenties. The three men waved the driver on, then coolly walked to the shelter of their sandbag emplacement.

As bits of concrete rained down, Pierre threw the taxi into gear and sped away, skidding around a corner, then weaving wildly through pedestrians running for cover. Lyons could not see the Mercedes, but Powell's voice returned as Blancanales turned up the receiver.

"Sounds like one-twenty mortars. Maybe two gangs banging at each other—hear that? That's the tube pop, but if they're the ones targeting the Green Line, they're firing way, way short. If they're trying to kill Christians. But then again, maybe it's Muslims fighting Muslims. Who knows?"

The woman's voice answered. "A profound analysis, Mr. Powell."

Blancanales switched on another receiver. An electronic tone wavered.

"What is that?" the taxi driver asked.

"It's the signal from a directional transmitter. Follow it and you'll find our man."

"You Americans!" the Lebanese marveled. "You have everything. Very modern. That is why your country is so rich. We want to be just like you."

Lyons looked around to the devastated streets, at the civilians cowering in doorways, at the militiamen waving rifles and RPG launchers. A Japanese pickup truck fitted with a Soviet 12.7mm heavy machine gun sped past. Weathered posters of Khomeini fluttered on the doors.

Lyons turned to the Lebanese taxi driver. "I think there's more to it than gizmos."

"Very modern and Christian. The world's most powerful nation. United by faith in Our Lord and Savior. When we liquidate all these filthy Mohammedans, we will also have modern nation, then we can prosper as the Lord intended for his Faithful—"

"Hey! Quiet!" Blancanales interrupted the discussion of culture and economics. "She's giving him directions...."

SPEEDING PAST THE ADDRESS, Powell scanned the rooflines and windows. He continued to the next street and wheeled a quick right, then a left. He went around the block and approached the tenement from the opposite direction. One block short, he slowed to a stop. Again he scanned the rooftops and windows and doorways for an ambush.

"Why would I lead you into a trap?" Desmarais demanded.

"To get me wasted."

In the distance, the mortar exchange continued against a background of hammering heavy automatic weapons. Sirens screamed through the center of the city. But on this street, only a few blocks from the squalor of the Sabra refugee camp, workers went to their jobs. Shopkeepers stood in their doorways listening to the outbreak of fighting a few kilometers away. Then they resumed placing their furniture and cloth and dishes in sidewalk displays. Other vendors continued putting out baskets of fruit and vegetables. Powell saw nothing indicating a trap.

"An ambush is not my purpose. I want your story, not your death."

"But wouldn't that be a story?"

"Why would your death be a story? You are nothing."

Powell looked at the young woman and laughed. "Out. You're coming with me. What happens to me, happens to you."

Taking his short Galil autorifle from the floor, he set it on the roof. He pulled off his coat, then buckled on a bandolier of ammunition and grenades. Now he looked no different than the Shia soldiers who had checked his pass at the roadblock. Desmarais raised her camera to photograph him.

"No!" He blocked the lens with his hands. He grabbed her sleeve and dragged her toward the tenement.

"But why not?" she protested.

"Don't you know American law? If an American citizen carries a rifle in a foreign army, he could lose his citizenship."

"But you are already breaking the law. You are a deserter from the Marines."

"Correction. I am AWOL. But that's only the brig. That's only a dishonorable discharge. If I get popped under the Neutrality Law, I can't go home."

"But still you serve with the militia. Why? What is the true reason?"

"Because...." Powell began as he watched every doorway. He stumbled over broken asphalt as his eyes looked everywhere—the windows, the balconies, the rooflines. Despite the cold, he felt the pistol grip of his Galil become slimy with his sweat. "Because I like the guys I'm with. They talk different, they act different, they eat different food, their Sunday is on Saturday, but you know, they're just like my people back home. Don't matter what the facts are, what's important is what it says in the Bible. 'Cept for them, it's the Koran."

"Interesting. I have never heard an American say anything like that. If you will give back my recorder, perhaps I'll interview you. There, that is the man's door."

"You don't want an interview with me, I'm nothing."

Powell glanced into a delivery van parked at the curb. He saw no one inside. He let the woman step into the stairwell first. Then he snapped a glance inside. Pausing on the stairs, she looked back at him.

"This is not a trap."

"We'll find out. Go on up to his door. Take a look."

She ran up the stairs. Powell stood in the doorway watching the street, watching her, listening. A musty smell, combined with the aroma of cooking food came to him. He heard her knock on a door and then call out in French.

"Je suis ici, Oshakkar. Avec l'autre Américain!" No answer. She called out again. "Oshakkar!"

A door squeaked. Boots rushed across concrete. Even as the woman screamed, Powell took two strides across the sidewalk and went low behind the bumper of the parked delivery van. He scanned the street, saw no one.

He heard men rushing down the stairs. In a squat, Powell pivoted and pointed his Galil at the doorway and the delivery van's back door flew open. He tried to block the door, felt the sheet-steel corner of the door gouge his left hand, then the door smashed into the side of his head and he went down.

Powell saw a blur of motion above him and boots jumped on his chest. He tried to point the short Galil, but a boot kicked it as he pulled the trigger, spraying a wild burst of high-velocity 5.56mm slugs whining off stones as the boot kicked again and other hands grabbed the rifle. Powell pulled the trigger again, emptying the 30-round magazine, then lashed out with the rifle, felt it hit. He released it and rolled away, coming up with his Colt Government Model.

Flat on his back in the street, he snap fired .45 ACP hardball into rushing forms, saw men go down. An AK muzzle flashed. ComBloc slugs tearing past his head, he fired, and a full-auto burst went wild, the muzzle sweeping in a circle as the gunner spun, slugs hammering steel, punching through other men. Powell scrambled for his own rifle.

Steel slammed the back of his head.

8

As the taxi coasted around the corner, bursts of autofire tore the street's quiet. Lyons saw passersby and vendors rushing for cover. Then he saw Powell, bearded, long-haired, roll backward on the asphalt. One militiaman kicked at the rifle in the ex-Marine's hands while another militiaman tried to twist the rifle away.

Lyons snatched his Konzak assault shotgun from the floor. Jerking back the cocking handle, he slid out the telescoping stock.

The taxi screeched to a stop, Pierre standing on the brakes, then he jammed the shift into reverse. The tires screamed and smoked as the cab hurtled backward.

"What are you doing?"

"Your work is done!" Pierre answered as he whipped the taxi through a circle and shifted again. "Those are Iranian Revolutionary Guards! They will kill him."

"Stop!" Lyons shouted, putting the 14-inch 'Urban Environment' barrel to the taxi driver's head. "Go back! He's an American. No one's—"

Staring into the 12-gauge muzzle of the Konzak, not watching the street, Pierre accelerated into a light pole. Steel screamed as the pole folded. The taxi went up the inclined pole, then fell as the pole broke. Spitting blood, Pierre pushed aside the muzzle of the Konzak autoshotgun and tried to aim a pistol at Lyons.

Blancanales threw an arm around the Phalangist's neck and jerked him back. Lyons grabbed the pistol. As Pierre clawed at the arm choking him, Lyons took two plastic loops from the pocket of his sports coat—disposable riot cuffs intended for Powell—and tried to cinch the taxi driver's hands together. Pierre clawed at Lyons's eyes. Lyons drove a fist into his gut. Pierre convulsed and in seconds, Lyons had the driver's hands linked together. Then he secured the man's hands to the steering wheel with the second riot cuff. Lyons jerked the keys from the ignition and ran from the taxi.

Sprinting past the corner and across the street, Lyons took cover in a fruit seller's doorway. He looked diagonally across the street to see Powell, on his hands and knees crabbing for his rifle. A militiaman in the uniform of the Iranian Revolutionary Guard brought down the steel butt of a folding-stock Kalashnikov on the back of the American's head.

Selective-fire Konzak gripped in his hands, Lyons charged the scene. Two Iranian militiamen lifted Powell. The ex-Marine slashed at their hands with a knife and they dropped him again. As the third Iranian swung his Kalashnikov like a club, trying to beat the struggling American into submission, a scream of rage turned them to face their doom.

"Die!" Lyons shouted, and he fired a wild scythe of full-auto 12-gauge, a storm of double O and Number Two steel ripping through the three standing

Iranian militiamen, arms flailing backward, bones shattering, steel balls punching through ribs and lungs and hearts, skulls disintegrating in a splash of blood and brains and tissue; the Iranians were corpses before impact threw them back.

Lyons's neoprene soles slipped in gore and he went down, sliding into the curb feet first, his momentum throwing him over. He smashed into the stone wall of the tenement with his shoulder, and his arm exploded with pain.

An Iranian with a pistol stepped from the tenement doorway. Lyons rolled onto his back and tried to raise his Konzak, but it fell from his numbed hand. Grabbing for his autoshotgun with his left hand, Lyons looked up at the bearded, sneering militiaman in the uniform of the Iranian Revolutionary Guard. The Iranian cocked the hammer of his pistol with his thumb and aimed between Lyons's eyes. In English, he pronounced a death sentence; "I send you back to the anus of Satan, American—"

With his left hand, Lyons pointed the Konzak and fired. The last shell in the autoshotgun tore away the Iranian's right leg at the knee, spinning him, the shot from the revolver going wild. Lyons, right arm numb and hanging dead at his side, dropped the Konzak from his left hand. He snatched the Colt Python from the hideaway holster at the small of his back and brought down the heavy revolver on the Iranian's head as he fell to the sidewalk. The Python's four-inch barrel came down again and again on the whining Iranian's face and skull until the broken-mouthed and bleeding man went slack.

"Powell!" Lyons called out. He pointed the pistol

around him, looking for targets. Wounded and dying militiamen thrashed on the sidewalk. But no one stood. "Powell! I'm on your side! Which side are you on?"

The ex-Marine had managed to find his Galil SAR. Dazed and smeared with blood, he struggled to change the magazine. He leaned back against the bumper of the van.

"Who are you? Are you—hey. . . specialist! Long time no see, thanks for stopping by."

"We got to talk to you. What exactly are you doing here?"

"Well, you know. Remember the last time we talked?" Powell dropped out the magazine of his Colt autopistol and slapped in another. "You said I should take a street-warfare class? Well, here I am. Taking graduate studies. But what are you doing here?"

"Agency sent us here to bring you back, dead or alive. We didn't know who you were. Now I don't know what to do. Gotta talk to you about what's going on."

Powell staggered to his feet. He looked into the van. This time he swung open the rear doors and surveyed the inside of the van, his Galil pointed, the safety off and his finger on the trigger.

On the sidewalk, Lyons rose to a crouch. He moved his right arm. Nothing broken or dislocated. He felt sensation returning. He went to the doorway of the tenement and listened. He heard only the ringing of his ears.

"Ironman!" Blancanales shouted as he ran up. The Politician carried an AK and wore a bandolier of

ComBloc mags across his sports coat. He tossed Lyons a black nylon bandolier, loaded with box magazines of 12-gauge shells. "Where's Powell?"

"Right here, secret agent," Powell replied. "Where's the other guy, the Wizard?"

"Over on the East side," Blancanales told him. He went to the doorway and peered in, then snapped his head back. He dropped down to one knee, then looked in again.

Powell called in. "Hey, *mademoiselle*! You there?" No one answered. "I had this reporter woman with me. She went up and knocked on this Oshakkar guy's door and then it all went very crazy."

On the sidewalk, the Iranian groaned and tried to move. Blancanales dashed across the doorway and examined the Iranian's destroyed leg. The ex-Green Beret medic pulled the belt from the pants of a corpse and applied a tourniquet above the blood-spurting tangle of flesh and cartilage and shattered bone. "He'll lose his leg, but he'll live."

"For a while." Lyons clenched and opened his fist. He swung his arm in circles, grimacing against the pain. Finally, his right hand functioning again, he buckled on the bandolier and reloaded his Korzak. "Let's go find that girl."

Powell scanned the street. People peered at the Americans from the cover of their doorways and shuttered windows. "She's either dead or gone, but let's go see. We gotta do this quick. I don't know which militia will show up to check out this shoot-out."

One at a time they dodged through the doorway.

No autofire came. With Lyons and Blancanales covering him, Powell sprinted to the top of the stairs, then they followed. The door to one room stood open. The door had been kicked open.

Inside, an elderly Muslim man in pajamas lay on the floor, a vast pool of blood around his slashed throat.

"I think they used this apartment to wait in," Powell told the others. "That apartment is Oshakkar's." He pointed to another door.

Blancanales checked the door for obvious booby traps. Then the others stood back while he kicked it open.

No one had remained in the one-room apartment. They saw only old furniture and murals. The murals were spread over all four walls, portraying scenes of idealized African men and women with Kalashnikov rifles standing triumphant on fields of dead pigs bleeding from thousands of bullet holes. The pigs had white skin and blue eyes. Some pigs wore the camouflage uniforms of the army, others the blue uniforms of police. Spray-painted slogans declared Victory To New Africa! The Nation Of Black Islam!

Blancanales, careful for booby traps, checked a closet and the drawers of a cabinet. He found only a dog-eared and stained magazine behind the cabinet. Every page had full-color photos of white women in scenes of torture and rape.

"Nothing. Except this." Blancanales dropped the magazine and wiped off his hand.

"Then where's the woman?" Lyons asked.

Powell laughed. "That imitation-French bitch reporter? Forget her. She came for a story and she found it. We got places to go, people to see."

On the sidewalk again, Lyons and Blancanales grabbed the moaning Iranian and dragged him toward the taxi. They heard a shot. Looking around the corner, they saw two teenage militiamen in jeans and leather coats, Kalashnikovs slung over their backs, unloading cameras and electronics from the taxi.

The riot cuffs still secured Pierre's dead hands to the steering wheel. Blood and brains had sprayed the windshield. The militia punks had put a bullet through the head of the handcuffed driver before looting Able Team's equipment.

Blancanales aimed his AK and fired, dropping both punks with ComBloc 7.62mm slugs through their brains. "We need another car."

Powell pointed at the van. "It has the keys in the ignition. Load up and follow me."

"Where?" Lyons asked.

"To my friends."

Posters of the Imam Moussa Sadr stared down from the walls. Shia militiamen—some in the mismatched fatigues of the irregulars, others in the OD uniforms of the Lebanese army—watched the Americans enter. They greeted Powell and stared at Lyons and Blancanales. Lyons received special attention. Clotted blood and filth stained his tailored sports coat and slacks. All the militiamen noted the unusual assault weapon the blond, blue-eyed American carried.

"Wait here," Powell told Lyons and Blancanales. "I'll talk to my friend."

The Marine continued into another office where

clerks typed at desks. Another clerk cranked a mime-
ograph machine. Powell went to a secretary and explained his visit.

Lyons grinned to all the militiamen. He turned to
Blancanales and said quietly, "Daniel in the lions'
den. Or maybe it's Lyons in the—"

A middle-aged, scarred militiaman interrupted
with a question in broken, accented English. "You
kill...massacre Revolutionary Guards?"

"Here goes...." Then Lyons answered in distinct,
short phrases. "Did not kill all. One lives."

The militiaman nodded, laughed. He told others
what the American had said. A young man spoke
quickly to the older man. The young man pointed to
the Americans, then outside. The older man asked
another question. "Why not kill all?"

"Information. Interrogate. Now others question
him."

"Yes, question, then kill. You Marine?"

"Only soldiers," Blancanales answered.

"But Americans, yes? Good. You kill Revolutionary Guard. We kill Guard. We kill Syrians, Russians,
PLO."

"But why do you kill them?" Blancanales asked.

"Marines friends. Revolutionary Guard kill Marines. We kill Revolutionary Guards."

Lyons nodded. "That's straightforward. Can't
argue with that logic. In fact, I nominate that man
for United States secretary of state."

Powell had returned. The scarred fighter pointed
to Lyons and questioned Powell in Arabic. Powell
answered and the man jumped up and grabbed
Lyons. Before Lyons reacted, the man embraced

Lyons and then slapped him on the back. All the others in the room laughed and cheered. Powell pulled the two Americans toward the inner office.

"What did you say?" Lyons asked, amazed.

"It's what you said, nominating Sergeant Azghar for secretary of state. All that old dude talks about is how the United States doesn't know its way around. How the U.S. should get smart. You most definitely made his day. Fact is, Azghar's got it right. The secretary of state don't know shit about Lebanon, and he ain't willing to learn."

Sayed Ahamed greeted them with embraces and handshakes. Today he wore a tailored suit and gold rings. Pomade glistened on his wavy hair. A French cigarette streamed smoke into the air as he gestured.

"Friends of my friend! He told me of his good fortune. Your clothes! I hope they are not ruined."

"I'm sorry, I didn't have time to change."

"To come here? Do not think you must be formal. I am dressed like this because of the negotiations. If I go in uniform, they think I'm a warlord. I must look like one of the despicable politicians to talk peace."

Both Blancanales and Lyons noticed the fatigues and web gear hanging on a coatrack. A Kalashnikov leaned against the wall.

"But you did not come here to listen to my complaints—" Ahamed lowered his voice. "The Iranians know Powell is my friend. They sent a message about the woman. They want him, not her. If he goes alone and unarmed, they'll let her go, they say."

Lyons looked at Powell. "You'll never come back. And neither will she."

"She has nothing to do with it. I need information, and she can lead me to a man who's got it."

"We'll question that prisoner, hear what he knows."

"Already happening," Powell told them. "They'll bring the information up real quick."

"We'll question him ourselves."

"No you won't, specialist. You may be a tough guy, but you just don't want to be involved in what's happening to that Iranian. Take my word for it. Ahamed's men do not like those Revolutionary Guards. Especially Iranians in partnership with Libyans."

"Libyans?" Blancanales asked.

Powell briefed them on the suspected plot between the Libyans and the Iranian Revolutionary Guard. "And Clayton got killed checking out that conspiracy. If I don't break it, I'm out of work. And the hit happens. Don't know who'll do it, don't know when or where, but that Libyan was looking at the President when he said, 'The sword rises.'"

"The President?" Lyons asked.

"Of the U.S. of A." Powell emphasized.

Powell reacted to the sound of footsteps outside and swung the door open as a militiaman raised his hand to knock. The militiaman relayed a report. Both Ahamed and Powell questioned the militiaman in Arabic.

Powell considered the information, nodding. "Good deal, we got our ticket. They won't know what hit them."

"What about the woman?" Blancanales asked. "Was the offer to trade her sincere? Will she still be alive?"

"The Iranian had information on that Oshakkar. He's an American black-nationalist psycho working with the Iranians. Now I don't need her at all."

"Dead reporters make for bad press," Blancanales cautioned. "Ask your man to question the Iranian about what they intend to do with the woman. Where she will be. Maybe we can get her out somehow."

"Too late, boy scout. No good deed. That Iranian went to paradise. You want in on this? You two and me and my friends against Libyans and Iranians and Black Muslims who want to murder the President of the United States?"

Lyons and Blancanales nodded, without a word canceling their assignment and accepting a new mission.

9

"Things have changed—"

"What?"

His back to the freezing wind, Lyons squatted on the rooftop of a West Beirut tenement with a view of the city and mountains to the east. He spoke with Gadgets Schwarz, who still waited on the roof of the apartment house where Powell lived in East Beirut, kilometers away. The absence of concrete and steel blocking the signals enhanced the transmitting and receiving range of the hand radio.

"We're in on a—" Lyons caught himself. Despite the encoding circuits of the hand radio, he decided not to risk briefing his partner. The Agency had access to the same equipment Able Team used. If the Agency directors learned that Able Team—after talking with the renegade agent they had been sent to Beirut to kidnap or execute—had decided to disregard instructions and join the renegade in an unauthorized counter-terrorist operation, Able Team might become three men without a country, outlaws.

"We're in on something interesting, that's all I can say."

"So what does that mean?" Gadgets demanded, his voice angry. "I'm up here getting frostbite while you're doing interesting things around town. What's going on?''

"Stay there. Continue monitoring. Watch for unusual—"

"You giving me orders, Ironman? This team don't work like that."

"I can't tell you what's going on, Wizard. I can't. When we get back, I'll give you the news."

"What's happened? What's going on?"

"Things have changed. Things aren't like what we were told. Remember the shoot-out in the desert with the *vatos*, the Twenty-third Street gang? We had that Texan who swore by .45 Colts?"

"A trip down memory lane...." Gadgets considered the information. "Oh, yeah! He was cool, but wasn't his name...."

"Yeah, it was and still is."

"That wasn't in the briefing."

"No, it wasn't. Another thing that wasn't in the briefing. That Texan's been specializing in street warfare lately, and there is no chance—repeat, zero chance—that we would have taken him alive. So be cool—" Lyons used the Wizard's jive "—and let me slide until I can brief you."

"Okay, okay. Cool it is. You don't know how cool, like I'm freezing."

"We'll get it done and get back to you. Later."

Lyons trotted down eight flights of stairs to a devastated street, where Blancanales and Powell and a platoon of Shias waited. He started for Powell's Mercedes. "Ready to go," he said.

"We're walking from here," Powell said as he moved from the side of the Mercedes, crossed the sidewalk and threw open the door to a shuttered shop. The Shias went first, moving quickly through the midday darkness along a familiar path. Powell waved a flashlight for Blancanales and Lyons as he spoke.

"The Iranians can't expect me to trade myself for the girl. But they know I'll show, seeing how they gave me their address. So they'll have ambushes set. Problem is, they're operating in Shia territory. And we know the sector better than they do. So they're going to die."

"You got another way in?" Lyons asked.

"That's it, specialist. No way I'm going through any front doors again today. That scene with the Revolutionary Guards was me at my most stupid. I thought that phony Frenchy knew what was going on and she took me straight into the trap. Ain't going to happen again."

The line of men moved through fire-gutted storerooms. Doorways had been blasted through the concrete walls to create a corridor leading through the buildings. Sometimes they walked through total darkness, sometimes through gray light filtering through artillery-shattered ceilings and walls. Rats skittered in darkness around them.

"Why do you call that reporter a phony Frenchwoman?" Blancanales asked. "Do you think she's traveling with a false passport?"

"Call her phony because she's got a Canadian passport and she calls herself French. That's about as phony as they come."

"A Quebecois?"

"That's it. Loser imitation French. Same as the

Maronites here. The Maronites think they're French. They don't speak Arabic. Always waiting for foreigners to come to their rescue, always willing to let foreigners die for their traditions, their privileges, their bigotry. The Crusaders, the Turks, the French, the Israelis, finally us Americans—we've all fought for those losers. And this is one American who ain't going to do it again."

"But the Christians fought the PLO," Lyons countered. "They can't be all bad if they kill those creeps."

Powell laughed. "The Shias fought them. The Druze fought them. The Americans, the Greek Orthodox, the atheists, the Syrians—they all fought the Palestinians. Even the PLO fought the PLO! But what do the Maronites do? They fight Palestinian women and children and old men. Against men with rifles, they call for the Syrians or the Israelis or the U.S. Marines."

One of the Shia militiamen waited for the Americans at the head of a flight of stairs leading down to a basement. "Okay, my friends," Powell said, "time to take the shortcut!"

Powell introduced the militiamen. "This is Akbar. He used to go to school in California. We work together all the time."

"Even if the Agency's uptight," Akbar added. "The money's all right."

"But that's all over if we can't get my job back," Powell said as he pointed down to the flashlights waving in the darkness below.

The stairs led down into a series of connecting basements. Water from broken pipes created black lakes stinking of sewage. The pointman led the line of militiamen and Americans through corridors, along fallen girders, across rows of crates. Sudden splashes startled the men, and rifle safeties clicked off. In the light of their flashlights, they saw a swarm of rats swimming through a flooded section. The flashlight beams sparked red from the hundreds of eyes of rats waiting on the far side.

Finally the Shias and Americans came to a steel hatch.

"Ready for a bad scene?" Akbar asked Lyons and Blancanales.

"The Iranians are on the other side?"

"Not that kind of scene, this kind—" As he swung open the door, the Shia militiamen covered their mouths and noses with handkerchiefs.

The smell hit like the shock wave of an explosion. The two men of Able Team choked and coughed as a warm wind, stinking of a miasma so fetid it seemed poisonous, rushed at them. But the Shias went through the hatchway.

Choking, nauseated, the Americans followed. In the dim light, they saw an underground garage filled with black sewage. Daylight came through a few street-level grills. The line of men hurried along a catwalk to the opposite side. They reached another door, threw it open and rushed into the semidarkness of a tunnel filled with pipes and electrical cables. The cold air of the tunnel felt like spring water on their faces.

Powell pointed to the closed door behind them and explained: "The plumbing got blasted in a car bombing years ago. There's about a thousand refugees living in the abandoned offices. They fixed the water lines, but no one can get down there to fix the sewer lines. So they just let it go. Must be the world's biggest cesspool. Been fermenting for maybe five years. And gangs use it as a body dump. Adds to the stink.''

"That—that was bad," Lyons said, laughing.

Blancanales finally got his breath back. "Is that our route of retreat if—"

"No way," Powell told them. "This tunnel will take us there. The Iranians probably have got an ambush right above us. We hit them, then walk out on street level."

"What about an ambush in this tunnel?" Blancanales asked.

The line of men slowed. The Americans heard whispers and quiet footsteps ahead. The flashlights went out except for one held by the first man.

"Probably not."

"Probably isn't good enough," Lyons said.

"You want point? Take it. Come on, specialist. We'll take point. First in line for the firefight."

Powell led Lyons forward. They moved by touch along the line of Shia militiamen. Ahead they saw the silhouette of a crouching man. As they approached he motioned them back and hissed a warning in Arabic. Powell translated for Lyons, "Akbar found a booby trap. . . ."

By the glow of his flashlight, Akbar secured a safety, then cut a trip line. He examined the device and hissed back to Powell. "One of ours. An old one."

They continued through the silence and darkness, Powell and Lyons in line behind Akbar as he followed an old map. From time to time, sounds came from the street above them, the faint thuddings of tires on asphalt carrying through the meters of stone and concrete.

Coming to an intersecting tunnel, Akbar switched off his flashlight. The men in line stopped as he listened. Lyons heard a coin jangle across steel and concrete. The flashlight beam returned and Akbar peered into the other tunnel. He compared the code stenciled onto the tunnel wall to the codes of the map, then continued.

The line followed. Now no traffic moved above them. They walked through an absence of sound, hearing only the sounds they made. Equipment clicking and knocking against rifles, every footstep, every breath echoed in the tunnel.

Akbar waved his light over the tunnel walls, noting stenciled codes. They passed another intersecting tunnel. Akbar ignored it. Then they came to a maintenance shaft. A point of light came through the manhole cover. In the darkness, the spot of light seared their eyes like a magnesium flare.

Squinting against the daylight, Akbar checked the maintenance shaft carefully. First he waved the flashlight beam into shadows and crevices. Finally he checked the rungs of the ladder. He pointed to a rung at face height. Lyons leaned close and saw a fine coating of dust on the rusting steel. Every rung had dust on it.

After another hundred steps they came to a narrower intersecting tunnel. Akbar and Powell checked the tunnel entrance carefully. They found nothing. Continuing, they followed the tunnel as it sloped upward.

A group of fighters had preceded them. Akbar found the dead where they had sprawled for years, their bones broken by high explosive and shrapnel, gnawed by rats. As the others crowded up behind him, Akbar pointed out the monofilament lines, the blast and scorch marks on the tunnel sides.

Apparently, a group of fighters—the skull fragments indicated five—had attempted to travel through the tunnel. They had encountered a clever booby trap. Set to be triggered by the first man, the monofilament ran back ten meters to a detonator that had fired two claymore-type charges. The blast had killed the entire line.

Someone had taken the serviceable rifles. Only one Kalashnikov remained among the old bones and rags, its sheet-metal receiver and magazine twisted together and pitted, the barrel bent, the wooden stock and fore grip torn away by point-blank shrapnel blast. Only bone fragments remained of the man that had held that rifle.

As Lyons walked carefully over the anonymous dead men—or women, no one would ever know—he saw bits of glittering shrapnel mixed with the bones and powdery rags. And the bones. . . he noticed that every bone had been scarred by thousands of rat teeth. Only the teeth of the dead lacked the marks, the hard enamel grinning from skulls and fragments of skulls and jaws.

Akbar moved slowly now, silently checking every possible position for a bomb, using his flashlight to examine every shadow and crevice. They passed panels of telephone circuits, unused for years. Akbar stopped to read the crumbling sticker on a panel door.

"This is the place," he announced quietly.

"Where are the Iranians?" Lyons asked, looking upward.

"If they're at the address they gave us, up there," Powell whispered. He continued to the end of the tunnel. An access ladder went straight up through a black rectangle. His flashlight showed the interior of a small room above them. "And I think they are because it's the same address the prisoner gave us. But who knows? Maybe they're up there, maybe not. Or they could be in a nearby building."

"What's above us?"

"A parking garage. It opens to the street and to the alley. There should be another garage across the alley. If there's an ambush, they'll expect us to come from the street. But we'll be coming up behind them—if they're on street level. Probably they're on the second and third floors, to be able to fire down."

"We'll go up first," Lyons volunteered, motioning toward Blancanales. "We've got the appropriate technology for this," he added, tapping his silenced auto-Colt.

Lyons and Blancanales slung their assault weapons over their backs and cinched the slings tight. With Lyons going first, they ascended the ladder into absolute darkness. Blancanales checked his silenced Beretta 93R and waited for his signal.

By touch, Lyons found an open area in a floor littered with broken concrete and bits of wire. Wires touching his head, scratching his face, he stood up in the darkness, listening, searching for light or form. Closing his eyes, he hoped for maximum dilation of his irises. But open or closed, his eyes saw only black.

He switched on a penlight. The glow revealed the gutted interior of a telephone circuit room. Deliberately destroyed with high-explosive charges, panels and wires filled the room. Torn cables hung from conduits.

Years before, someone—perhaps one of the five dead found in the tunnel—had blocked the door with a length of steel pipe jammed like a crossbar between the two panels bracketing the door. The lock and door handle had been shot out. Scratched paint showed that an attempt had been made to force the door open. But the attempt had failed. Judging by the bones in the tunnel and the rust on the shot-out lock, the room had not been opened for years.

Lyons listened at the door. He heard nothing. He returned to the tunnel entry and hissed to Blancanales. His partner joined him in seconds.

"Might be a dead end," Lyons whispered.

"We'll know when we open the door."

Slowly and silently they raised the length of steel pipe. Blancanales stood by to jam it back into place. The door was hinged to open inward, and Lyons slowly eased the door open a hand's width.

Rats squealed and skittered, claws scratching at the door. Concrete and trash spilled through the opening. A rat hurtled into the small room, squeaking, running wildly through the wires and metal fragments until it dropped through the trapdoor. Below, they heard the Shias curse and stomp.

Points of light appeared at the very top of the opening. Dust swirled in the faint light. Lyons and Blancanales smelled the stink of rotting garbage and generations of rat filth. More trash and debris fell through as Lyons continued opening the door. He ignored the rats leaping against his body and scratching over his boots. He could hear the Shias in the tunnel as they continued to stomp on rats.

Ahead of him, Lyons saw a wall of trash. Through the years, trash and debris had been piled against the door, covering it completely. Faint daylight glowed through the top layer of papers and filth.

Now they heard sounds outside—the jangling and crashing of a truck on the street came to them, but no voices.

Moving the square steel box of a wiring panel to the doorway, Lyons stood up and tried to look over the top of the wall of trash. As rats skittered and ran on the other side, he gently cleared a hole through the papers and rotting garbage. He saw a street-level garage. He continued clearing aside the trash.

Autofire hammered.

10

Lyons fell back as Blancanales attempted to close the door against an avalanche of trash and filth. But the debris blocked the door.

On the other side the bursts of automatic-rifle fire continued.

But they heard no slugs hitting the trash or door. They waited, listening.

"They're not shooting at us," Blancanales told Lyons.

Standing on the box again, Lyons looked outside. He saw no one. Another burst shattered the quiet, the autofire echoing in the garage. Lyons heard no ricochets or voices, or the sound of running. He dug through the trash and broken concrete, then crawled into the light.

Scanning the area, he saw debris from years of explosions and fighting littering the garage. Burned-out wrecks blocked the alley exit. Two new Japanese panel trucks sat parked on his left. Then he heard voices coming from a flight of steel-and-concrete stairs.

A dead militiaman sprawled on the stairs, blood draining from wounds. He wore the fatigues of the Iranian Revolutionary Guard. A rifle fired, the noise coming from somewhere above the dead man.

"Pol! Get the others! It's clear."

Lyons scrambled out. He pulled out his auto-Colt, checking to see that it was cocked and locked, and ran across the garage to the stairs. He looked up and quickly dodged back as an autorifle fired.

But no slugs came at him. He looked at the dead man. The Iranian had been shot in the back.

Looking across the garage, Lyons saw Blancanales lead the line of men out of the trash pile. Blancanales and Powell ran across the garage to join him. Akbar directed the platoon of Shia militiamen to cover the street and alley exits.

Lyons went up. At the first landing he went flat on the concrete and looked up the next flight of stairs. He saw an open fire exit with the door gone, but the low angle denied him a view of the corridor beyond. He heard voices, then kicks against a door. A rifle fired once.

He went up the next flight of stairs on his hands and knees. Stairs squeaked behind him as weight stressed the steel framework. He looked back, saw Blancanales. Lyons continued to the top.

Peering into the corridor, Lyons saw two Iranian militiamen fire their Kalashnikov rifles at a closed door, punching the door and the walls on each side with lines of 7.62mm ComBloc. Then they ran at the door and kicked it. A rifle inside fired one bullet out, splintered wood and plastic flying from the door. The Iranians scrambled for cover.

Lyons braced his silent Colt on the top stair. Thumbing the fire-selector down one click to semi-automatic, he sighted on the head of the Iranian farthest from him and squeezed the trigger.

The Iranian moved. As he raised his rifle to his shoulder, the .45-caliber hollowpoint slammed into his left cheek at three hundred meters per second, the upward trajectory of the impact-flattened slug tearing away his eyes and half his face. The force spun him back several steps; he was still alive, blood and fluids spraying from his opened skull.

A second slug caught the other Iranian low in the back of the head, killing him instantly as the expanding hollowpoint liberated a devastating shock force of kinetic energy to explode his skull.

Motioning Blancanales and Powell up, Lyons ran through the corridor. He continued past the door to the lobby of the office building. Rusting steel grills covered the long-ago-shattered plate-glass windows. Moldy papers, rifled files and charred furniture littered the lobby. Vandals had spray painted Arabic slogans on the gray marble walls. Everything not burned had been smashed. Only twisted metal and broken glass remained of what had been an abstract sculpture of colored glass rising from the lobby to the mezzanine.

Nothing moved on the mezzanine level. Lyons saw no one on the stairs. He heard nothing in the building.

Lyons turned at the sound of footsteps. Blancanales and Powell stood on each side of the bullet-splintered door. Shia militiamen ran past the door. With the universal hand signals learned by fighting alongside soldiers of many languages, Lyons pointed to where he stood, indicating the interior of the high lobby in a wide sweep of his arm. The Shias nodded. One man squatted against the walls and watched the lobby, his AK rifle ready. The other Shia ran down the stairs to the garage.

Lyons returned to the door. Powell glanced at the two dead Iranians, then at the splintered door.

"Who's in there?" Powell asked in a whisper.

Lyons shrugged.

"Mademoiselle!" Powell shouted in his most nasal Texas accent. "Is that you shooting in there? What is going on?"

"Who is it? Is that you, American? Tell me your name!" a female voice demanded, the voice cracking. "Tell me, identify who you are!"

"This is you-know-who come to rescue you. Mr. Nothing."

"Captain Powell!" the woman shouted. They heard sheet metal squeaking. A weight shifted, then crashed. The door opened and Anne Desmarais looked out. Her face bore the marks and blood of a beating. She held a Kalashnikov. When she saw them, she tried to open the door completely. It banged against metal. She struggled with the door and sobbed. "Oh, finally. Thank you, oh my God I prayed...."

Blancanales spoke slowly, soothingly. "Do you have the door blocked, miss? Do you need us to push the door open? Set that rifle's safety so we don't have an accident. Do you know how to set the safety? That lever on the right side, push it all the way up. That one, good. Step back, we'll push the door open."

The combined force of the three Americans forced a filing cabinet back. Holding the Kalashnikov in one hand, her coat closed with the other, the young

French woman sat on a desk top, crying. She wore nothing under the long coat. Her knife-cut sweater and jeans lay in the trash on the office floor. Blancanales went to her immediately, easing the autorifle out of her hands.

"They raped you?" he asked gently.

Desmarais nodded.

As Blancanales soothed the woman, the others checked the dead and wounded. A dead Iranian lay face down on the floor, his fatigue pants around his knees. A moaning man sprawled against a wall clutching a massive wound. Unlike the Revolutionary Guards, he wore the tailored suit and stark white shirt of a diplomat. He sat in a pool of blood, moaning, his eyes watching the Americans.

Powell laughed. "That's First Secretary Baesho, of the Socialist People's Libyan Arab Jamahiriya, also known as the Land of Khaddafi Duck. How are you doing, first secretary?"

"I am a diplomat!" the man responded tersely. "I expect the respect due a man of my position. You will take me to a medical facility immediately!"

Squatting in front of Baesho, Powell grinned into the suffering man's face. "I won't do nothing to you. Unless you cooperate. Then maybe we'll help you out, you miserable bag of pig shit. You had Clayton killed. You tried to get me. Why?"

"You are violating international law—" Baesho began.

Jerking back the diplomat's head by his greasy hair, Powell pulled him to his feet. The diplomat screamed and struggled, his bloody hands clutching at Powell.

Pink intestines bulged from the gut wound.

"See that man over there, First Secretary Pig Shit?" Powell pointed to Blancanales. "That man's a medic. That man can save your life. Talk or I let you die."

Baesho vomited blood. Powell dropped him and the diplomat fell on his face. Blood spread around his head as he vomited and choked. He stopped breathing. Shudders racked his body.

Powell jerked his head up and screamed into his face. "Don't die! Don't.... Ah, shit! He's dead. And I wanted to kill him. Here's one for the road, first secretary."

Drawing back his booted foot, Powell released the shuddering man's head and drop-kicked him in the face with enough force to flop him backward. Against the wall, Baesho took a long last gasping breath, his eyes fluttering and rolling. His eyes fixed on Powell. Powell drew back his boot for another kick.

"Quit it, Powell," Lyons told him. "It's pointless."

Powell ignored Lyons and kicked the diplomat again, snapping the dead man's neck.

"One more thing...." Flipping off the safety on his Galil, Powell fired a burst into the dead man's face, spraying brains and bone. He fired again and again until he destroyed the man's head.

Lyons jerked the Marine captain back. "Quit it!" he shouted.

Powell changed the autorifle's magazine. "Hey, specialist. This is my business. That Libyan was in on the barracks bombing. Until you spend a week or so looking for pieces of friends—men that had wives and kids and babies they never got to see and futures they never got to live—until you do that, you can't tell me to quit. I could kill that creature a thousand times and it wouldn't be payback! You understand?''

"I understand we lost the chance to question him. Now we've got nothing but corpses."

"He wouldn't have lived long enough to question."

Akbar came into the ruined office. "We found the ambush. We killed them all."

The woman spoke quietly. "His briefcase. There, over there. Inside the briefcase—"

Lyons snapped open the gold-trimmed leather attaché case. Inside, he found passports, stacks of one-hundred-dollar bills still in bank wrappers, and folders. The folders contained airline tickets and complete sets of identification—worker cards, university-student-union identification, and miscellaneous photos of families and places.

Lyons turned to Akbar. "You killed the Iranians outside? All of them? Not one escaped?"

"A wipeout," the Shia militiaman told him. "Totally."

"The tickets are for flights to Mexico," the young woman explained. "All these..." she paused to think of an obscenity, then spat out the word, "Iranians! That one would have sent them to Mexico. There was a Nicaraguan here. They did not know I spoke Spanish. They talked and laughed at what the Iranians did and then the Nicaraguan left. They were raping me, they thought I was unconscious. I tricked them. That one, the Libyan, he went out with the

Nicaraguan, and the Iranians went out. Then that one came in to rape me again and he did not see me take a rifle...."

His voice soothing, slow, Blancanales asked, "Can you tell us what they discussed? What do they intend to do in Mexico?"

"No!" Desmarais looked around at the men. "I know but I will not tell you unless you take me to Mexico with you. This is my story."

"Miss, you're all beat up," Blancanales told her. "You need rest and a doctor's care. I don't think it will be possible—"

"No! I need no doctor. I can go. And only if I accompany you, will you learn the information you need."

In the front room of Akbar's family home, surrounded by stereo and video systems, the Americans enjoyed a traditional meal as they studied the contents of the first secretary's attaché case. Akbar urged food on his American guests. Gadgets, who had finally received a radio call to give up the rooftop wait, drank hot tea.

"It was cold up there!"

Blancanales laughed. "I don't think you would have liked where we were, either."

"Far-out system you have." Gadgets pointed at the shelves of entertainment electronics. "But why five color televisions and all the VCR decks. Looks like Cape Kennedy in here."

Akbar only smiled. "My family is in the business," he said noncommittally.

"I eat with my hands?" Lyons interrupted.

"Right hand for eating," Akbar instructed. "Here you can use your left hand for picking up the bottles and dishes. In other countries they're more strict about the left hand. The best idea is to watch what they're doing and do that. That is a chili! Oh, man...."

Too late, a handful of rice and lamb spiced with green chili seared Lyons's mouth. He grabbed a bottle of orange pop from the table with his sticky right hand. The bottle shot from his hand, but he grabbed it in midfall with his left and he gulped pop. "Hot! Hot...hot...." he said breathlessly.

"When I was in L.A.," Akbar said to the Americans, "everyone thought they could burn me out with Mexican food. Not me, man. I ate it all."

Lyons sucked down breath after breath, then drank more orange pop. "Not you. I understand. They grow super-jalapeños in Lebanon?"

"Looks like we'll be going to Mexico," Powell told them.

"Is that the final destination?" Blancanales asked. "Or one more stop in the zigzag?"

"That's where all the tickets go. And this—" Powell pointed to a series of tickets. "There's a sequence of arrivals. There's no sequence in Amsterdam or Paris. The Iranians were to get off in Mexico City and call this contact. One man at a time. If Mexico was only a stop, they'd get off the plane, then go to the bus station, zip on to the next place."

"Makes sense," Lyons admitted. "But so what? Maybe it's a zigzag, maybe it isn't. But that's where their contact is. We take him, he takes us to the next stop."

"There goes the Ironman," Gadgets added. "Cutting through all the machinations and mystery. Don't talk about zigzags to him. All he sees is straight lines."

"You want to spend three weeks analyzing this data?" Lyons demanded. "Maybe wait for a Congressional Resolution? We're leaving for Mexico, immediately."

"And how does our dear Mademoiselle Desmarais figure in your plans?" Powell asked.

"She doesn't. She wants a story. Chances are she didn't hear anything. She just wants to stay in the game."

"Like you say, maybe and maybe not," Powell responded. "I know she's got information. Now that I'm a good guy, maybe she'll tell. I'll have hours and hours on the plane to talk."

"If she can travel," Blancanales cautioned. "She could be hurt in ways she doesn't even realize. I hope she has the intelligence to listen to the doctor if he wants to hospitalize her."

"I know her type," Powell said, laughing. "She won't listen to anyone. Akbar, look at this one. Think you could pass?" Powell flipped a passport to his Shia friend.

Akbar wiped off his hands and studied the passport's photograph. "Am I that ugly?"

"It's that joker's beard. You'll have to say you shaved, but the forehead and eyes match."

"You're sending him to Mexico City?" Blancanales asked. "If the contact's gotten word of the killings...."

Lyons nodded. "Yeah, they'll try to hit him. Either way, you make the connection."

"I don't like that idea!" Akbar protested.

"We'll be there," Lyons told him. "We'll back you up."

Akbar's elderly manservant ushered in Anne Desmarais. She had put on makeup to cover her bruises. Though she walked stiffly, painfully, she carried a suitcase. "When do we leave?"

Powell looked to the others. "Any minute now, if—"

"We'll make our own plans," Lyons interrupted. He looked to his partners.

They nodded their agreement.

11

Via satellite-relayed long-distance telephone, Blancanales talked with Captain Soto of the army of Mexico. In the months since Able Team—aided by then-Lieutenant Soto—attacked the forces of the Fascist International, politics had played a central role in the life of Soto. The officer mentioned arrest and imprisonment followed by reinstatement and promotion to captain. But he held no bitterness for the North Americans. He laughed at the difficulties caused by Able Team's previous visit to Mexico.

"I am now famous. A hero," Soto declared. "I will tell you many stories when you visit."

"And we will tell you a story. Perhaps you will have a role to play."

"Oh? You come on business?"

"Important business. Can you meet us at the airport?"

"Certainly! Of course. It will be my pleasure to—"

"Can you meet us *before* we go through Customs?"

"Oh, I understand...I will think of something. Leave the plane last. Do not follow the crowd into the terminal."

"We will see you. If there is a delay or if we must change flights, we'll call again."

"Good. I look forward to your visit."

After breaking the connection, Blancanales paid the desk clerk in dollars. He received his change in Greek currency. He did not bother to count the change. Able Team would be on Cyprus only another hour.

Gadgets and Lyons waited outside the tourist hotel in a limousine. Blancanales hurried through the freezing rain and joined his partners in the warmth of the idling Mercedes.

"You talked to him?" Lyons asked.

"He said he can help us—"

"Great." Lyons signaled the driver to continue to the airport.

"But you know," Blancanales continued. "He's had serious problems since we were there."

"He still in the service?" Gadgets asked.

"He was in prison. Now he's back in the service. With a promotion to captain."

Lyons laughed. "After this, maybe he'll hit major."

12

Knives flashed in the firelight. Choking on their own blood, the Syrian soldiers kicked and struggled in the grip of the Iranians. Rouhani watched the Syrians die, then motioned his Revolutionary Guards on to the next sentry position. Two of his men stayed in the sheet-metal shack to dispose of the bodies and stand watch.

The others ran through the gray pall of falling snow. The mercury-arc floodlights spaced along the perimeter guided the Iranians to the next entry shack. They approached slowly, listening to the Syrians inside talking around the fire. Rouhani signaled two of his Guards to go inside. He and the others waited outside, like shadows in the swirling snow, their knives ready.

Greeting the Syrians like friends, the two Revolutionary Guards stepped up to the fire and warmed their hands. One Guard took American cigarettes from his coat. He offered the cigarettes to the Syrians and the soldiers each took one. As the two sentries leaned down to the fire to light the cigarettes, the other Iranians rushed in with their knives.

Again, the Syrians died quickly.

Rouhani left his Guards at the post. Alone with his thoughts, he walked into the gray swirl of blowing

snow to the village. His heart hammered with exulta-
tion. Tonight he finally took command of the strike
against the satanic Americans. No longer would the
Syrians control the rockets.

He had never believed the Syrians would actually
kill the American President. They hid behind dip-
lomacy and foreign relations and negotiations.
Cowards! How can a *believer* negotiate with Satan?

Had not the Syrians waited at their nation's fron-
tiers for years, facing the Jews but never attacking?
Did not the Syrians tolerate for years the Americans
in Lebanon? Did not the Syrians possess the Soviet
missile systems, only for the missiles to stand unused,
never launched against the Jew enemy or the Americans or the other enemies of the Faith?

Now the Syrians made rockets to attack America.
But would they ever launch the rockets?

Rouhani would not wait for the answer. Tonight,
under the cover of this storm sent by Allah, while the
Syrian officers and technicians holidayed in Damas-
cus, he took the weapons of doom from the Syrians.

On the streets of the village, his Guards saluted
him from doorways. His men held the offices and
workshops. Rouhani did not know what holiday
took the Syrians back to their capital. He did not
care. He honored only the holidays ordained by the
Prophet or declared by the Ayatollah. Let the Syrians
celebrate their orgies of alcohol and sensuality—the
thought sickened him. The video machines of por-
nography, the American and European films in the
theaters, the imported luxuries, the Syrian women in
tight pants and shimmering fashions, their bodies
scented with exotic perfumes, their faces painted,

their lips red and pouting, like a promise of paradise....

No! He refused to think of the venereal filth, the corruption on earth. He must direct his thoughts only to destruction, to the rain of doom on the creatures of Satan.

The Americans would be there when the rockets fell, the scented women in their revealing gowns, their breasts hot, rising and falling with every trembling breath as they watched their foul President of America taking his oath of depravity and dominion over the people of the earth.

Destroy them! With explosives, with white phosphorus, with the nerve gases! Rain down the fire of death on them, rip their flesh and let their polluted blood drain into the polluted earth of satanic America. Cleanse the earth of their sin and evil!

Hallucinations of sex and death flashing against the swirling snow, Rouhani ran down the long ramp to the underground factory. Inside, he stared around, his eyes still focused on the erotic visions generated within his mind as his men crowded up to him.

"Leader! The trucks are ready..." one shouted.

"Have you cleared the sentries from the gates?" Rouhani asked.

"Leader...are you wounded?"

Rouhani shoved away the Guards attempting to help him. He brought his thoughts back to the immediate moment. Striding past his men, he surveyed the workshop.

Set deep under the abandoned fields of the village, protected from Israeli or American air strikes by

steel-reinforced concrete, the factory contained rows
of machines. Diesel trucks were parked in the center
aisle. Steel gurneys, straining under the load of
240mm rockets, stood alongside workbenches, where
the Syrian technicians had left them. At the far side
of the concrete cavern, more racks of the BM-24
Soviet artillery rockets stood against the walls.

"Why not those rockets?" he demanded of his
Guards. "Why do we leave them?"

"They are not modified, Leader. Today Dastgerdi
talked with all the Syrians. They talked about what
rockets were ready and what ones were not. We put
only the finished rockets in the trucks."

"How can you be sure they are ready?"

"The Syrians marked the rockets."

"How many?"

"Almost a hundred. Four launchers, ninety-six
rockets."

"And the transmitters? And the warheads? Are
the rockets prepared with explosives and poisons?"

"Yes! The Syrians were very proud. They bragged
of their quick work."

Rouhani laughed. "Start the trucks!"

THE CONVOY OF DIESEL TRUCKS and cars drove
through the night, north to Baalbek, then northeast
toward Lebanon's coast city of Tripoli. Papers
forged by the Libyans identified the Iranians as PLO
reinforcements for the city. The documents declared
the cargo as weapons for PLO and Syrian armies stationed around the city.

But before they reached the city, Rouhani directed
the convoy off the highway. The cars and trucks

bumped over a frozen, rutted road to an improvised airstrip. There, PLO agents hired by the Libyans transmitted a signal to the approaching cargo plane.

"Where is First Secretary Baesho?" Rouhani asked the Palestinians.

"He is delayed."

"By what?"

"There has been much fighting in Beirut. The telephones do not work. We could not speak with the embassy."

"But what of the plane? Does this—"

"We continue. We have our instructions, the plane will come as scheduled."

"When? There can be no delays now."

"It is off the coast. It waited for our signal."

"But we must be out of Lebanon today!"

"Be patient. It will be only a few minutes."

Rouhani stared into the sky. The eastern horizon grayed with dawn, the irregular line of the eastern mountains black as the storm-darkened sky. Rouhani knew that if he and his Guards did not leave Lebanon today, they risked the revenge of Syrians. Syrian troops occupied all of northern Lebanon. Thousands of Syrian soldiers surrounded Tripoli. Syrian units patrolled the coast to the west and the borders to the north and east. Syrian forces manned the emplacements to the south.

One radio message could mean the extermination of Rouhani and his Guards.

The noise of the engines of the cargo liner stopped his fears.

Before daylight, the Iranians loaded the plane with the rockets and launchers.

Then they flew west. To destroy the President of the satanic empire of America.

FROM THE WARMTH AND LUXURY of his armored limousine, Dastgerdi watched the Sahel Mountains blur past. He considered the reports.

Repeated radio messages to the base in the Bekaa had not been answered.

Syrian units manning roadblocks had reported two trucks and trailer loads of rockets in transit to Tripoli.

A radar station in Tripoli had reported the intrusion of an aircraft of unknown nationality. The aircraft crossed the coast, disappeared into the foothills, then reappeared after less than an hour, flying due west. Radar tracked the aircraft over the Mediterranean until it passed out of range.

Then came the reports from the Syrian Defense Ministry. The radio operators speculated that the failure of communications during the night had perhaps been caused by the storm. But the reports from the checkpoints and the radar station had been confirmed.

The slowing of the limousine interrupted his thoughts. His Syrian-army chauffeur turned from the highway to the narrow road leading to the ruined village. Snow covered the familiar landscape. Beyond the abandoned fields and pastures, storm clouds hid the peaks of the mountains.

How had the night's storm affected his project? Had the hate-crazed Rouhani seized the opportunity of the holiday and the breakdown in communications? What would Dastgerdi find at the village?

The insanity of the Iranian Revolutionary Guard captain threatened the greatest project of Dastgerdi's career. Had he correctly predicted the actions of the Iranian lunatic? Had his informers in the gangs of the Islamic Amal correctly reported the Libyan efforts to subvert the project and seize leadership?

And what of the KGB? Had they somehow learned of the operation? In the chaos of hatred and insanity and nationalistic fervor, had one of the outsiders sold information about his project to the KGB?

Doubts tore at Dastgerdi. Any one of the foreigners involved in his project—the Iranian Revolutionary Guards, the Libyan diplomats, the fanatic Shias of Islamic Amal, the mercenaries—might betray him. Though he had compartmentalized the duties and commands, one breakdown might lead to another and another and finally to the end.

When he saw the gates to the village standing open, unguarded, he knew.

At the sentry shack, he stepped out of the limousine and went into the corrugated steel shelter of the sentries. The frozen corpses of the Syrian soldiers sprawled beside the ashes of the fire, their blood a red ice on the mud.

Dastgerdi ran outside. He wanted the chauffeur to see his alarm and confusion. He looked fifty meters away to the other sentry positions on the perimeter. Nothing moved.

His greatcoat flapping, he ran back to the limousine. His voice trembled as he commanded the chauffeur:

"To the factory!"

"Is there a problem, Colonel?"

"Don't question! Go!"

The driver spun the tires, accelerating through the snow. As they raced through the shellfire-shattered village, Dastgerdi saw nothing—no Syrian soldiers, no smoke from fires, no bored Iranians milling about. Near the entrance to the underground workshops, Dastgerdi shouted, "Park here! At the top of the ramp—wait."

"Colonel, it could be dangerous."

"That is my worry!"

Dastgerdi ran down to the entrance. The rolling steel doors stood open. Snow had settled on the concrete floor of the cavernous underground complex.

A quick look told him that four launchers and ninety-six rockets had disappeared. Truck tires had marked the concrete floor with wide lines of mud and frozen slush. The forklifts had left other lines. A confusion of footprints indicated where the Iranians had crowded around the diesel trucks.

But the Iranians had not taken the rockets and launchers stacked at the far end of the underground factory. They had only taken the ninety-six rockets fitted with *dummy* guidance units. The Syrian technicians had marked those rockets as finished, and the Iranians had taken the rockets away...most likely to America.

Glancing back to the entry ramp, Dastgerdi saw the chauffeur waiting in the warmth of the limousine. Only then did Colonel Dastgerdi allow himself a laugh.

He had played a game of intrigue with fanatics and lunatics, and he had won.

13

A sea of lights appeared on the horizon. As the stew-
ardesses hurried through the jetliner's aisles checking
safety belts, Powell woke Anne Desmarais. She had
slept through all the flights, taking pills at the airports
and sleeping, only waking for meals and drinks and
more pills. Powell attempted to make conversation,
but she told him nothing.

Yawning and stretching, wincing at the pain of her
two-day-old bruises, she ran her hands through her
hair and blinked at the view of Mexico City. She stared
at the horizon-to-horizon lights, not comprehending
what she saw.

"We're there," Powell told her. "How do you
feel?"

"Sleepy."

"You mean, doped."

"Where is your friend?"

"Up there in the middle of the plane. Don't look for
him. We could have some of the bad guys on the
plane. Not too late to back out of this. You could give
me the information and take a plane back to Canada.
You wouldn't even need to leave the airport."

Desmarais shook her head. "This story is very important to me. It will be a major step in my career. I
can't stop now."

"Hey, there won't be no story. Not if things go straight."

"Oh, yes. There is a story, of that, I am sure. Because I know the story!"

"Like those two ragheads who were in the photo? The Iranian and the Syrian army officer? What's the story on those two?"

"You will learn."

WAITING UNTIL ALL THE OTHER PASSENGERS left their seats, the three North Americans finally joined the line of travelers leaving the jumbo jet. Service workers in yellow uniforms slipped through the line of passengers and moved among the rows of seats, picking up papers and plastic cups, emptying ashtrays. One worker made eye contact with Lyons.

"This way," he said.

Lyons turned to his partners. They also recognized the sharp Nahuatl features of Captain Soto. The North Americans followed a step behind Soto to the passenger bridge. But instead of continuing to the terminal gate, Soto opened a door. They stepped into the dawn chill and hurried down an aluminum stairway to the asphalt. The ground personnel very deliberately ignored the three North Americans.

"There!" Soto shouted over the roar of jet engines, pointing to the open doors of a catering van. "What does your luggage look like?"

Blancanales answered. "Three sheet-metal shipping trunks. All green with brass trim. Identical."

"What names?"

"Guerimo Soto. All the same."

Soto closed the van's doors. The driver gunned the

engine and sped around the parked jetliners. The noise of the jet engines was cut off when the truck swerved into a hangar. The driver turned to them.

"We will wait here for the captain. You must not move or talk."

Sitting in the back of the van, Able Team listened to the activity around them. Workers shouted to one another, metal containers crashed along conveyor belts, horns beeped. Finally, tires squealed to a stop behind the van.

Grunting with the weight, Soto pushed the three green shipping trunks into the back of the van. He got in and pulled the doors closed. Then the truck sped out of the food service hangar.

"Now what, my friends?"

"We need to meet an American." Lyons glanced at his watch. "He's arriving approximately right now on another plane. He's with a Shia militiaman who's on our side and a Canadian woman reporter who isn't."

Soto instructed the driver. As the van circled to the passenger entrance of the international terminal, Able Team briefed Soto on the Iranian-Libyan plot against the President of the United States. Gadgets did not join in the discussion. He opened his trunk and assembled electronic gear.

"And they have come to Mexico? You are positive?"

Blancanales nodded. "We have the tickets and passports. We assume they plan to enter the United States from Mexico."

"Then we can mobilize all the security forces necessary to defeat the terrorists. When you called, I thought this was perhaps another...ah, political problem, as it was in the other action."

"Murder is murder," Lyons interrupted. "We only chase murderers. I don't care what their politics are. Fascists, commies, scumbag dopers, they get wasted."

"As you said when we fought the International. However, the politicians have other opinions, as I learned. But I will tell you of my education later—here is the terminal. Who makes the contact?"

"I will," Blancanales offered. "I speak the language, I don't look like a tourist—"

"Here, in your pockets." Gadgets passed Blancanales a hand radio. "And here's a DF so we can follow you. A minimike. Anything else you can think of?"

"Extras for others."

"You got it."

"Do not take a pistol into the airport," Captain Soto warned.

Blancanales nodded. As he pushed open the van's door, he gave his partners a quick salute. "Stay close."

Then he hurried through the lines of taxis and cars. Weaving through the crowds of travelers, he scanned the terminal for Powell, Desmarais and Akbar. And he searched for surveillance, watching for eyes watching him.

But the thousands of faces in the crowds defeated his efforts. Anyone could be surveillance: the elderly Castillian man, the North American hippies in *huraches* and *huipiles*, the dark-featured *Mexicana* traveling with her children, the security guard armed with the .45 auto-Colt. Blancanales had only his anonymity as a mask.

The crowds surging through the entry prevented him from taking full strides. Unconsciously he continued searching as he flowed with the terminal's masses, his eyes always scanning, looking for the unusual or the unlikely. Yet he realized professional surveillance agents would avoid any distinguishing appearance. He eased along with the other people, his head turning from side to side.

He checked the flight arrival and departure notices. The plane carrying Powell, Desmarais and Akbar had arrived on schedule. He went to where incoming passengers exited customs and took a seat.

After five minutes, Akbar appeared. He wore sunglasses and three days' growth of beard. Blancanales rushed through the arriving passengers, rudely shouldering some, pushing past others. He bumped into Akbar and slipped the coin-sized units of a directional transmitter and a miniature microphone into his coat. Then Blancanales stood at the exit and watched as the other passengers cleared customs.

Powell and Desmarais emerged two minutes later. Powell saw Blancanales and continued past without a word, Desmarais at his side. Blancanales waited a few seconds, then followed them through the terminal.

Akbar went to the pay phones, Powell and Desmarais to the car-rental booths. Blancanales casually joined them at the rental counter. He waited until the clerk turned away, then dropped the miniature directional-finder transmitter and the minimicrophone into the pocket of the Canadian woman's coat. The Canadian did not notice.

"We came in without a problem." Blancanales made a pretense of reading a brochure as he spoke. "They're outside, ready to go."

"Akbar will give us a signal when he knows what goes," Powell told him. "So you watch us. Stay away until we leave."

"Then I'll jump in." Blancanales folded and pocketed the brochure, then went to the foreign-currency exchange. After converting the American dollars and Lebanese pounds in his pockets to pesos, he turned to see Akbar walking to the exit. Akbar went outside to the curb and waited, ignoring the taxis and hotel limos.

Hurrying back to the van, Blancanales stepped inside and threw off his coat. He buckled on the shoulder holster for his silenced Beretta 93-R. "It's in motion. Watch Akbar, he's at—"

"I see him there." Lyons said, pointing. "What's going on with Powell?"

"As planned. He's renting a car. I'm on my way," the Politician said as he opened the vehicle's door.

Outside, Blancanales surveyed the traffic lanes of the terminal. He noted the pickup and drop-off points, the taxi waiting zones, the lines of rental cars. He walked quickly to a traffic island a hundred meters from the rental cars.

From where he stood, he had a view of Akbar waiting, of Powell and Desmarais sitting in the rental car, and of the parked catering van. Powell saw him standing on the traffic island and flashed his headlights.

Situation covered. But as he waited Blancanales never let his eyes stop, always searching the sidewalks and traffic lanes for sign of a pattern in movement, a pattern that meant ambush or kidnap or surveillance. He watched the crowds behind Akbar. He watched the arriving traffic, looking inside the cars and trucks, watching for any odd detail.

After fifteen minutes, a panel truck stopped in front of Akbar. The driver leaned out his window and spoke to the young Shia. Blancanales saw Powell reach for the ignition of the rental car. As Akbar got into the panel truck, Blancanales felt the hand radio inside his coat click. He answered with three clicks of the transmit key.

The panel truck accelerated past Blancanales. He memorized the make of the truck, the license number and the face of the driver.

Seconds later, Powell braked to a stop at the traffic island. Blancanales got in the rear seat. As they accelerated away, Blancanales looked back and saw the catering van weaving through traffic. He slouched down below the level of the front seat and keyed his hand radio.

"Any conversation?"

"They're jiving in Arabic," Gadgets reported. "I'll put the walkie-talkie up to the receiver. Let Powell listen, maybe he can translate...." Gadgets's voice faded away.

Then came the scratchy, twice-transmitted voices from the panel truck ahead. Blancanales held the hand radio behind Powell.

"He's quizzing him—" Powell began.

"I thought you didn't speak Arabic," Desmarais said.

"Don't really. Just listening for what I recognize.

He's...he's asking him what's going on, who he knows. Akbar's saying he doesn't know. The other guy's asking about Iran, what town he comes from. This does not sound good.''

Traffic slowed. When the cars stopped, vendors rushed from the curbs to offer candy and newspapers and prepared food. One *indígena* woman offered eggs to the commuters. Brilliant against the soot-gray morning in her threadbare blue satin blouse and hand-woven skirt, her throat flashing with the traditional strands of gaudy beads, she went from car to car, almost running, holding three eggs between her fingers like a magician demonstrating a trick. One driver called out, *"¡Quiero una docena!"* A whistle and a few sharp words in a language Blancanales did not understand brought two barefoot children from the curb with more handfuls of eggs. The woman and the driver bargained, closed the deal, counted eggs and money in less than thirty seconds, then the traffic moved again.

On one block crowds of workers crossed the boulevard and filed down the stairs of the subway station. Blancanales looked through the rental-car window to see people everywhere, workers hurrying to the subway, vendors selling goods, boys waving newspapers, motorcyclists weaving between vehicles.

A young man stepped out in front of the stopped cars and spit out a spray of flame.

"What is going on!" Powell raved.

"This is Mexico City," Blancanales said, laughing.

The signal changed and traffic moved again. Drivers and passengers threw pesos to the fire breather. Blancanales tossed out a Lebanese five-pound note he'd kept.

The panel truck ahead of them veered to the right, swerving across two lanes of traffic. A diesel truck blocked Powell.

"Straight ahead! We're on them," Gadgets shouted through the hand radio. "Make a right turn at the next street. We'll give you directions. They say anything about spotting you?"

As Blancanales pressed the transit key, he saw the catering truck make a right turn. Powell leaned on the horn and switched lanes, daring a motorcyclist to hit him. He spoke into the hand radio, "If he's Iranian, that's the way they drive. Get closer and stay there."

"We're not in an unmarked vehicle, you know," the Wizard replied.

"Risk it. Otherwise, Akbar's gone." Powell whipped the car through a skidding right-hand turn and raced up the block. A double-parked truck slowed him. Sounding the horn, he swerved to the left, almost crashing head-on into another truck and accelerated again. "Which way? Which way!" he shouted.

"Wizard! Did they turn?" Blancanales asked.

"Straight ahead. Or—"

Powell floored the accelerator. The engine stalled. "God dammit! Move car, move it!" Grinding the starter, he raced the engine, then shifted into drive. The car hurtled across a boulevard full of traffic. Brakes screamed, and the car flashed past the bumper of a cattle truck, then they raced up the next block. Skidding through a right turn, then an illegal left, Powell merged with the boulevard's traffic.

Two cars separated them from the panel truck. Powell slowed. He let a car swerve in front of him. Finally, a light brought traffic to a stop.

As at all the other intersections, the vendors left the curbs en masse, waving their goods. Blancanales saw boys and women around the car.

Metal tapped the windows, and Blancanales looked into the cylinder of a suppressor pointed at his face. He looked to the other window, saw another hand holding another suppressed pistol. The gunmen stood close against the car, their bodies screening the sight of the pistols from the other cars.

"Open the door, Mr. Powell," an accented voice said.

"They've got the pistols," Blancanales said loudly, knowing that the miniature electronics in his pockets would transmit the information to Gadgets. "There's nothing we can do...."

"Very intelligent," the voice commented.

Blancanales opened a back door. A squat gray-haired man in an overcoat slid into the back seat. His pistol touched Blancanales's gut.

"*Buenas días*, my American friends. I am Señor Il-lovich, cultural attaché of the Soviet Embassy. It is a pleasure to welcome you to Mexico City."

14

"I'm going to kill that Soviet shit," Lyons muttered as he snapped back the slide of his auto-Colt. With a hollowpoint in the chamber, he set the safety. "Have your man pull up close. First chance I get, Cultural Secretary Illovich of the KGB is dead meat."

Captain Soto shook his head. "You cannot kill a diplomat."

"Why? Political problems? He's got a pistol. Say he shot himself."

"Ease off, Ironman." Gagets switched from channel to channel on his receiver, monitoring first the Arabic conversation in the panel truck, then the talk in the rented car.

The Soviet's voice droned on, calmly reassuring the Americans. "It is for the best that we join you. This Iranian driver seems to be an excellent operative. I see that you have a gun, American. Allow me to take it, for the sake of safety. We do not want a misunderstanding. Thank you. You do realize, that if you continued in your pursuit, that Iranian driver would have noticed your car—"

"He doesn't know about us," Lyons commented.

"Unless he knows and wants to trick us," Gadgets countered. "Listen—"

"We have several vehicles, Mr. Powell," the Russian continued. "Let the truck go ahead, my men will follow."

"I can't let that truck out of sight! My friend's in there," Powell shot back.

"I will maintain contact with my radio... and with whom do you maintain contact? Señor... I do not know your name."

"Damn, he's got the Pol's Beretta and now he's got the radio!" Lyons cursed. "He knows there's someone else out here."

In the rental car, Blancanales touched the hand radio in his coat pocket. "This radio?"

"I do not mean my radio." With his free hand, Illovich touched the earphone plugged into his left ear, then pointed at the hand radio in Blancanales's coat pocket. Blancanales did not move. The Soviet applied pressure to Blancanales's ribs with the suppressor. "I promise to return it also."

Blancanales laughed softly as he passed the radio to the Soviet. Illovich smiled, showing off a set of perfect white false teeth.

"You laugh at the promise of a Soviet diplomat? You Americans.... " Illovich studied the hand radio. He pressed the transmit key again and again. "And, for your information, I will also return your pistol. Does that surprise you? You do not yet understand.... "

Gadgets's faint voice answered the clicks, static pops and scratches almost drowning his words. "This is center unit. Come in unit three. Report position. Speak loudly, you are at extreme radio range."

Only a few car lengths behind Illovich, Gadgets rubbed his hand radio's microphone against his beard stubble as he whispered again. "Report position. Speak distinctly...." He crumpled a piece of paper. "Extreme range...."

Illovich passed the radio back to Blancanales. "So you are not alone. I return the radio, as I promised, but I also promise to shoot you if you attempt to prematurely contact your CIA pals."

"CIA? Me?" Blancanales asked, incredulous. "Why do you accuse me of that?"

"Do not deny it, Señor American. It would not be amusing. And you, miss. Are you also an operative of the Central Intelligence Agency?"

"No!" She spat out the denial. "I am a citizen of Quebec and an independent journalist. I am researching the CIA, but I would never associate with those—"

Powell laughed. "Unless you could get a story."

"—that gang of international criminals."

"What's your opinion of the KGB?" Powell demanded.

"Of course you are CIA. All American journalists are spies."

"I am not American! I am Quebecois!"

"So you speak bad French? American, Canadian, what is the difference? All foreign journalists spy for the CIA. Have you not read the great newspaper of my country, *Pravda*? 'Pravda' means 'truth.'" The Soviet laughed at his own irony. "And you, Mr. Powell. You were an operative, but you are not now, correct?"

"News gets around, don't it?"

"Think of your sudden liberty as an opportunity. I know of you, I know your talents. A man of your

skills and experience would not suffer if he worked for
the security agencies of my country. Put the political
conflicts of our countries aside, consider the benefits.
You would work with other professionals, at the command of professional leaders in the government. No
more impossible directives from senile movie actors
attempting to win votes with television spectacles. Instead of racing from place to place, attempting to correct problems that have no solutions, you could work
to preserve world order, a world without war, where
the Party leads a joyous humanity into the—''

"Gulag. The Siberian concentration camps. The
firing squads and the unending march of the living
dead into the pits.''

Illovich shrugged. ''Severe measures regrettably
must sometimes be taken. But those are only for
criminal elements. Here, Mr. Powell. I brought an application with me. Take it, it is yours. Study it.''

Without taking his eyes from the traffic ahead,
Powell slapped away the paper. ''Who are you? Some
kind of commie comedian? Never heard such shit.''

"Ah, yes. It is wrong of me to make the offer in
front of others. It was my way of putting you all at
ease. It was perhaps a joke. But consider it. When you
go back to the United States, you return to a very
uncertain future. And that is the truth, if I—''

Illovich went quiet, listening to a report through the
earphone he wore. ''Mr. Powell, accelerate. The truck
is stopping. They appear to be transferring him to
another vehicle.''

"What's going on?''

"Make a right turn at this boulevard. This may be a
very perilous moment. Mr. Powell, you must be

ready. If there is a difficulty, you must identify my men as friends, or there may be a very unfortunate misunderstanding with your Lebanese friend. There, you see the truck? It is stopping...."

On a quiet side street lined by evergreens and flowers, the panel truck slowed to a stop behind another truck. The driver threw open the door and ran to the second truck. He pointed back to Akbar.

Two Iranians stepped from the truck, pulling pistols from under their coats. They aimed at Akbar and fired.

Powell floored the accelerator. He sped past the first truck, then whipped the car to the right, hitting the contact man and a gunman, tearing away the truck's driver-side door, the three impacts coming in one crash, the men and the door flying into the street.

Standing on the brake, Powell slammed the car into reverse and shrieked rubber. A shot from the second gunman banged off the hood, Desmarais screamed, then the panel truck blocked the gunman's aim. Powell jammed the brakes again, skidding the rental car to a stop.

Converging on the scene from opposite directions, two sedans braked to a tire-smoking stop. Men in dark suits—Soviet gunmen—ran from the cars shouting in Spanish. *"¡Policía! ¡Policía! ¡Alto!"*

The surviving Iranian turned. As he raised his pistol to aim, the dark suits fired. The gunman staggered back, his pistol falling from his hand, his legs spurting blood. He fell against a wrought-iron fence.

Akbar came out the back of the panel truck. Powell shouted at him. "Over here!"

In the back seat of the rented car, Blancanales

shoved the suppressor against the seat. He felt the pistol jar as Illovich fired a round into the upholstery.

Desmarais turned and sprayed Illovich with tear gas. She held down the button of the purse-size canister with one hand as she opened the door with the other. "Americans, get out! We must run!" Akbar shouted.

As Powell and Desmarais abandoned the car, Blancanales and Illovich, both choking, coughing, with watering eyes, fought for the pistol. Finally, Blancanales twisted the autopistol out of the Soviet's hands.

A Soviet gunman leaned into the car and pointed a gun at Blancanales's face. Breathing hard, his eyes streaming tears, Illovich took the silent pistol from Blancanales.

"Thank you." Illovich gave a command in Russian, and the Soviet ran after Powell and Desmarais. "A waste of time. They will not get far," Illovich said as two Soviets dragged the leg-shot Iranian gunman to a car.

At the corner, another car screeched to a stop, and a Soviet enforcer pointed a submachine gun at the running couple. Powell and Desmarais sprinted across the street, trying to make the safety of the boulevard. The Soviet fired a burst in front of them, the slugs pocking a rough-stone wall. They stopped. The Soviet motioned them back to where Illovich waited.

At the rented car, another Soviet agent quickly and expertly searched both Powell and Desmarais. He took the tear-gas sprayer from the woman and handed it to Illovich. Then Powell was ordered to start the car and follow the other cars away.

His eyes still filled with tears, Illovich examined the tear-gas sprayer. "Do all American girls carry these?"

"I am not—" Anne Desmarais began.

Illovich silenced the woman's denial with a spray of tear gas.

"Is that an official residence?" Lyons asked as they watched the last car turn through the gates of the walled and guarded grounds of a city estate.

"I know it is not their embassy," Soto answered. "I will get the information later, but first we change this truck for cars."

"What else can you get?" Gadgets asked.

"We must decide at what level this operation will proceed," Soto answered. "We can keep all this within my unit, which will unfortunately limit what we can do. Or we can go to my superiors and explain the threat to your President. If we do that, we will have all the resources of the security forces. However, that may take time."

"That's not the only trade-off." Lyons took a last glance at the estate as the catering truck passed. "We go official, it takes time. It also takes it away from us. Your people won't let us operate. Then if the Iranians get across the border, we've got to go official up there, too. More time. More limitations. I say we only need a few cars. Once we get Powell and the Politician loose from those commies, we're ready to go. Wizard?"

"Get a mobile home. With a shower. A bullet-proof mobile home. With a color TV. And a video machine and some videos and some movies on tape. And—"

"Kill the wish list," Lyons said, laughing. "You ain't a senator yet!"

"You asked."

"There's a limit."

"Then come up with a panel truck. I want to park outside the people's palace back there and monitor the place."

SCREAMS ECHOED FROM THE BASEMENT. As if he had not heard, Illovich poured tequila into a tumbler. The screams continued. The two Americans glanced to one another. Illovich watched the Hispanic as he passed the tumbler of clear liquor to the American agent.

Illovich tried to guess the man's ethnic background. Mexican? Puerto Rican? Central American? The man could be one of the three Colonel Gunther had encountered the previous month when the combined force of American operatives and Mexican mercenaries smashed through the structure of Los Guerros Blancos. In a week of smash-and-run attacks, the gang of killers had first destroyed the dope gangsters and Mexican-army units ruling the opium fields of the Sierra Madres, then slashed through the maze of criminal-military-political alliances to attack the headquarters of the Fascist International operations in Mexico.

That attack had very nearly ended Illovich's most ambitious scheme: the penetration and control of the highest offices of the Fascist International by the Soviet Union.

Throughout the previous decade, Soviet KGB officers had succeeded in infiltrating thousands of agents into the security services and death squads of many Latin nations. These agents believed they served the American CIA, or the Salvadoran government, or patriotic Argentine exiles, or any one of many other reactionary groups. At the instructions of their neo-Nazi officers, and with the aid of the KGB, these thousands of agents annihilated the moderate political elements of Central and South America. Teachers, students, labor organizers, priests, progressive politicians, compassionate businessmen, idealists, evangelists—anyone not subscribing to the Stalinist diktat of the Soviet Union, died. Forewarned and sheltered by the KGB, only the cadre of Soviet agitators and manipulators avoided the death-squad assassins. When the oppressed people of Guatemala, El Salvador and Nicaragua inevitably rebelled against their feudal overlords, Soviet-trained-and-financed cadres emerged from the universities, slums, and army barracks to lead the revolutionaries.

But the death-squad agents remained in the lower ranks of the Fascist organizations. The Soviet Union needed agents who attended the conferences of the leaders. Through years of patient work, creating identities and arranging "victories" to demonstrate his agent's intelligence and loyalty, Illovich had finally succeeded in placing an East German operative in the highest military-political circles of the Fascist International. Colonel Jon Gunther, supposedly born in Paraguay, supposedly the ambitious son of a German family dedicated to the ideals of the Thousand Year Reich, had attained the coveted position of the International's military-liaison officer to Mexico. Gunther had served to integrate the actions of the Mexicans within the hemispheric strategy of the Fascist International. He had shuttled between the capitals of the Americas, coordinating and often initiating the responses of the Pan-American elite—the wealthy, the oligarchic Families, the transnational corporations— to the rising storm of nationalism and democracy throughout North and South America.

Then the three Americans and their mercenaries had almost defeated Illovich's ambitious plot. If Gunther had not escaped. . . .

Yet from the near-disaster, Gunther had wrenched a significant gain: the recruiting of one of the Americans. Gunther had offered the blond leader of the operatives, the one called "Ironman," gold and a leadership role in the Fascist International if the American became an agent in the employ of Gunther. The "Ironman" had accepted and helped Gunther to escape. Though the Ochoa gang had immediately re- captured Gunther, the American had fulfilled his commitment. Or had it only been a trick?

Illovich must know the truth. As he poured drinks for the captured Americans, a thousand plots and countermeasures swirled through his mind. Somehow he must contact and then test the blond American known as "Ironman." Could these American agents lead him to the other man? His long joke with the employment form in the car had been a test. Somehow he must break through their resistance.

Holding the bottle to an empty glass, Illovich glanced to the Lebanese.

"And you, my friend?"

Akbar shook his head.

"Oh, forgive me. I forget. Your faith."

They sat in the library of the house. Shelves of books rose from the floor to the ceiling of the room. Heavy velvet drapes, smelling of dust and age, covered the windows. Desmarais paced the room, studying the framed prints on the walls, the titles of books, the pre-Conquest sculpture displayed on the tables.

"I'll take a refill." Powell put his tumbler on the old desk.

Illovich flashed his startlingly white false teeth. "It is not often you have the opportunity to drink with the opposition."

"Yes, the pleasure of drinking with the opposition," Powell mimicked. "Even if it's this strange cactus vodka, right, Illovich?"

The Soviet laughed. "Cactus vodka! How true. I had not thought of it like that. Is that what tequila is called in Texas?"

"We call it a lot of things. Like, deadly. Like, white lightning—"

A piercing, shuddering wail interrupted Powell. The captured Iranian screamed until he sobbed down a breath and screamed again.

"Oh, yeah! Do it to him!" Powell laughed and gulped tequila. "You Soviets know how to treat an Iranian. If I join up, will you put me in charge of questioning mullahs? I got some ideas I want to try out."

"You joke." Illovich touched an intercom key. He spoke quickly in Russian.

An aide immediately rushed into the library. With a long pole tipped with a hook, the aide closed the heating and cooling vents near the ceiling. Then he closed the vents in the floors. The Iranian's screams became distant, only a whisper in the background as they talked.

"Not often—not lately, that I get a chance to

drink," Powell continued. "Hanging out with Shias, you know. Bottle of tequila could get you shot. Or whipped. Muslims are just crazy when it comes to alcohol and things like—"

Blancanales interrupted Powell. "Secretary Illovich, why are we here? Why the drinks and polite conversation? Why aren't we down in the basement?"

"Yes, yes. To business. Señor, you may appear Latin, but you certainly demonstrate the impatience of an American. To business. I would have thought I have made my interest and intent obvious."

Illovich paused to sip his vodka and consider his words. "As you know, the Soviet Union leads the world in the quest for peace. No, do not taunt me with your sarcasm. My words are true. Though your nation and the other capitalistic, imperialistic nations provoke us, we restrain ourselves, we wait, we attempt to negotiate, we never fail to demonstrate our peaceful intentions.

"We now face a problem that, though not of our making, if it comes to pass, will surely confront the world with unprecedented displays of American militaristic aggression. We are confident we could counter the American actions, but of course it would be much better if the crisis did not occur at all—"

"Illovich! Okay! What the hell are you talking about?" Powell demanded.

"Why...the Iranians, of course. They came to kill your President. We can't allow that. I am offering all the assistance of the Soviet Union to prevent that terrible occurrence from threatening the peace of the world!"

15

In a truck parked a few blocks from the walled mansion, Gadgets Schwarz monitored the three audio sources transmitting from inside the estate. He heard the sounds of clothing rustling, of footsteps, of voices speaking Russian and English and Spanish. Once he heard Powell and Akbar speak quickly in Arabic.

He mentally traced the locations of the minimikes as he listened.

The transmitters that Blancanales had placed on the Canadian woman did not move. Apparently, she had taken off her coat. He heard the sounds of a bed squeaking, then water running. Minutes later, he heard a door close. No more sound came from that microphone as the sound-activated circuits shut off.

Akbar seemed to be pacing in a room. Gadgets heard coins clinking against the disk of the transmitter as the Lebanese walked. Once when Akbar had spoken to Powell, Powell hissed him quiet. Powell knew the Soviets would be monitoring all the conversations of their guests.

Blancanales knew Gadgets listened. Blancanales could not risk a one-way conversation using the minimike in his pocket because of the Soviet microphones in the house, but he made a point of speaking to Illovich and Powell, commenting on the decor of the house, the rooms, the views from the windows, the angle of the sunlight in the garden.

Every comment helped Gadgets visualize the interior. He took notes, sketching the house and grounds. The sketches became diagrams. If Gadgets, Lyons and Mexicans had to break into the compound to rescue Blancanales and the others, they now had a map.

Then he heard the sounds of doors slamming, of people running through the rooms. A Russian-accented voice shouted, "We go now!"

"You got the information from the Iranians?" Powell asked.

"Yes. We have. We go now."

"Finally...."

"Where are they all running to?" Blancanales asked. "Why are they bringing out the cars? Five cars? Do they think they're going to a battle?"

Gadgets signaled the Mexican lounging across the front seats. Because the Soviets had taken Blancanales's hand radio, Gadgets and Lyons could not risk using their radios. Instead, they used the radios of Captain Soto's antiterrorist unit. The Mexican spoke into his handset, relaying the information in words Gadgets recognized as Nahuatl—the pre-Castillian language of Mexico—and street jive.

"They are ready," the Mexican reported to Gadgets.

Sounds came from the minimike in the Canadian's room. Gadgets turned down the other frequencies and heard the door open, then the woman's quick footsteps. Slow, heavy footsteps accompanied her.

Bus noises from the street forced Gadgets to turn the monitor up louder. Listening, he heard the deep voice of Illovich, speaking French.

Gadgets flipped the switch of his cassette recorder. As Illovich and the Canadian spoke, the cassette machine recording their French dialogue, Gadgets checked his other equipment. He switched on the directional-impulse receiver and listened to the steady beeps on three frequencies.

Illovich and Desmarais continued talking.

What do they have to talk about, Gadgets wondered. He watched the cassette turn inside the recorder. Don't know now, but we'll know later....

Finally their conversation ended. Gadgets heard the slap of heavy footsteps receding, followed by the sound of Desmarais gathering her camera and tape recorder, then a rustling sound as she slipped on her coat. He faded down her frequency and turned up the minimikes on Blancanales and Akbar.

He heard car doors slamming. Engines gunning. Illovich issued instructions in Russian.

Gadgets turned to his driver. "This is it!"

POWELL AND AKBAR rode in a new Dodge with Illovich. Their driver followed the line of cars through the traffic of a *viaducto*, one of the expressways cutting through the seemingly endless sprawl of the world's largest city.

Ahead, in a Mitsubishi passenger van, Blancanales rode with Desmarais and several Soviet gunmen. They saw the young woman turn around to snap a photo of the Dodge. A gunman blocked the lens.

"Why you letting that reporter come along?" Powell asked.

"I could ask the same question of you, American. You brought her to Mexico."

"Freedom of the press, you know. Told me she'd cut me in on the money."

"Behind the sacred principle, a profit. You Americans are not so difficult to understand."

"Hey, Ruskie, what about you?" Powell replied. "I doubt if the President knows that you of the evil empire is his friend. But you're helping him. Fact is, you're probably helping both sides. Tricky Ruskies. You all make snakes look like higher-life forms."

Illovich smiled. "I know it is difficult to understand. To think that my country would protect a government that hates us. Incomprehensible. Personally, I find you Americans incomprehensible. Your people, your government, your leaders—impossible!

"Your senators and congressmen, your President, and your President's advisors, they believe they are blessed. They walk about as if all the world loved them. Only your President has the minimum of protection. And even he, a malcontent with a twenty-two-caliber pistol shot him!

"Why must they endanger themselves? Do they realize their insatiable urge to touch the citizens, to pose and strut before the crowd threatens world peace? Are a few votes so important? Is voting so important? I think it is ironic that the Soviet Union must defend democracy from its malcontents. Oh, well," Illovich said, shrugging, "anything for peace."

"They ain't our malcontents. They're Iranian Revolutionary Guards," Powell responded.

"True. My apology. They are not Americans. But they are a product of the United States of America. The occupation and subjugation of Iran by the CIA and their puppet the Shah produced the Revolutionary Guards. Now they come to take revenge for the—"

"Yeah? What about Afghanistan? Maybe the Big Red in the Kremlin's next for a hit squad."

"Afghanistan is another example. Fortunately we Soviets and the progressive Afghan masses united in brotherly opposition to the forces of—"

Powell cut off the Soviet. "Those police cars with us? Or is the show over?"

"They are with us. This may become very sticky, you understand."

"Oh, yeah," Powell agreed. "I know about Iranians. Wish I didn't."

STAYING LOW IN THE BACK of the panel truck, Gadgets took the Mexican walkie-talkie and buzzed Lyons. "Those police are with the commies."

"Organized operation."

"No doubt about it."

"Any word where?"

"They're not saying anything. Powell's rapping with the El Numbero Uno Ruskie, talking jive politics. Don't mean a thing. Picking up Russian from the other car. Soto know Russian? Or French? I taped Quebecky talking with El Rusko."

"I'll ask."

After a moment, Captain Soto spoke from the walkie-talkie. "I studied French in the university."

"But can you understand it?" Gadgets asked.

"I worked in a tourist shop as part of an investigation. I will attempt a translation of the tape."

Gadgets put the cassette recorder to the walkie-talkie and played back the conversation between Illovich and Desmarais.

"So what're they saying? I know it concerns us, she used our names."

"Please play the tape again. The Russian speaks French. The woman's accent is very difficult for me."

Gadgets played it again. "You got it that time?"

"I cannot give you a literal translation. But the woman works for the Russian. The Mexican police will kill the Iranians and your friends. The woman will photograph it and distribute the story. I did not understand everything they said, but—"

"You're positive? They're going to off—"

"There is more. The Soviet questioned the woman about you *norteamericanos*. Your descriptions. Your names. She told him you were called 'Politician,' 'Wizard,' and 'Ironman.' He asked many questions about you."

"So now he knows about the rest of us. Put the Ironman on the talkie."

"I heard—" Lyons announced.

"We've got to stop them, like now."

"Hit them first. And fast," Lyons said.

"That's my man. Always ready with the plan."

IN TRUTH, Lyons had no plan. He did not know the location of the Iranians. He did not know how the Russians would mount the assault on the Iranians. He did not know the role of the Mexican police.

But he knew the assault would end with the executions of Blancanales and Powell.

Rather than allow the unknown elements to paralyze his reasoning, to create overwhelming doubts and inaction that would condemn his friends to death, he turned his thoughts away from the unknowns and concentrated on his assets in the situation.

As he rode through the midday traffic of Mexico City, the noise of thousands of cars and trucks beating at his concentration, he mentally listed the positives.

The minimikes relaying the conversations in the Russians' vehicles.

The directional transmitters.

The limited weaponry of the Soviets and Mexican police. He knew they had pistols and submachine guns, but he doubted if they had armament matching the modern military weapons of Able Team and Captain Soto's antiterrorist squad.

Surprise. The Soviets thought they had eluded the American force tracking the Iranians.

And more important, knowledge. He knew the approximate strength of the combined Soviet and Mexican force. The Soviet leader knew nothing of the Americans following and almost nothing of the Iranians.

A realization came to Lyons. The Iranians had lost three men, two dead and one captured. They might think all three had been killed, but a cautious leader would assume their location had been compromised.

The Iranians had two options: they could run or they could stay and fight.

In Beirut, the Iranians and Libyans had set ambushes. Why not in Mexico City?

But would a firefight advance their plot to assassinate the President? The Soviets and Mexicans might find no one at the location.

Lyons thought through the possibilities. He visualized the line of Soviet and Mexican cars approaching the Iranian position. He ceased to be Carl Lyons of Able Team and considered the approach as the Soviet leader would. Then he considered the action from the viewpoint of the Iranian leader.

No one plan could anticipate all the variables. Lyons blanked out his doubts and fears. He forced his mind to formulate a plan. Then he briefed the others.

THE LINE OF SOVIET UNMARKED CARS and Mexican police cars caravanned through an industrial district. Listening to a Soviet gunman talk via walkie-talkie with other Soviets, Blancanales scanned the gray warehouses and filthy streets. Diesel trucks parked in alleys, others backed up to loading docks. Laborers crowded around the trucks, unloading boxes and sacks by hand, sweat flowing from their bodies. At other docks, skiploaders shuttled between trucks and the stacks of crates in the warehouses. The smells of rot and diesel fuel and food cooking flooded through the windows of the van.

"What's this area?" Blancanales asked Desmarais.

She did not meet his eyes. "I have no idea."

The Soviet gunman next to Blancanales jabbed him with the muzzle of a pistol. "Why you talk?"

Blancanales spotted a street sign and said the name. "You recognize that street? Where are we?"

"Why don't you ask the driver?"

"And I thought you were familiar with Latin America."

The Canadian only shrugged. The gunman jabbed Blancanales again and the American went quiet. He turned in the seat and looked behind them.

Blancanales saw cars and panel trucks leaving the line, taking side streets and alleys off the boulevard. He resumed his pretense of talking to the Canadian.

"We're close. They're splitting up. Must be intending to approach from different directions. But us and Illovich and the others are staying together."

The Canadian turned and looked. Smiling with a secret knowledge, she glanced at Blancanales and smirked.

The Dodge carrying Illovich, Powell and Akbar stayed behind Blancanales and Desmarais. The Dodge and the passenger van continued along the boulevard another block, then turned right.

"Must be close now. Here we go. . . ."

"Are you nervous, American? Why do you talk so much? I thought secret agents were strong and silent. You chatter."

Blancanales looked back again. He saw a pickup truck leave the boulevard. Two young Mexican men in stained shirts sat in the cab, laughing with one another. The pickup truck gained on the Dodge.

Then another car and panel truck left the boulevard. The pickup truck accelerated to pass the slow-moving Dodge and passenger van. Blancanales saw the other vehicles gaining. Watching the pickup truck pass, he saw the young Mexican men eyeballing Desmarais.

The Soviet gunmen watched the speeding truck. A walkie-talkie squawked. Then, in the back of the pickup, a Mexican sat up with a silenced Heckler and Koch MP-5.

Even as the 9mm slugs shattered glass, hammered sheet metal, tore through the bodies of the Soviets in the front seat, Blancanales grabbed the wrist of the gunman next to him. He forced the pistol against the front seat as the pistol jumped again and again.

Then the van crashed.

CROUCHING IN THE BACK of the panel truck, a round in the chamber of his CAR-15, Gadgets watched the pickup and the taxi cab gain on the Soviets. The pickup accelerated to parallel the Mitsubishi van. The taxi cab accelerated to pull alongside the Dodge.

Voices came from the Mexican walkie-talkie as units of Captain Soto's force raced to their positions on the other streets.

Gadgets slap-checked his gear a last time, touching the Velcro closures of his Kevlar-and-steel battle armor, the bandoliers of magazines and grenades, the fit of his sunglasses.

Ready to go. Gadgets snapped his bubble gum and watched as the Mexican in the back of the pickup killed the three Soviet gunmen in the front seat of the Mitsubishi passenger van. He saw Blancanales struggling with the Soviet next to him. The multiband receiver blared sounds of panic and shooting from the three frequencies of the minimikes.

Fifty meters ahead, Lyons leaned from the window

of a taxi cab. He pointed the fourteen-inch barrel of the Konzak out the window of the taxi and put a 12-gauge blast through the back left tire of the Dodge carrying Illovich. The tire exploded and flapped on the rim. Lyons put a second blast through the front left tire.

Jumping the curb, the Mitsubishi crashed into a parked truck. The pickup truck glanced off a streetlight pole and skidded sideways to stop, its tires smoking and screaming.

But the driver of the Dodge accelerated, aiming the bouncing, tire-shot car at the pickup. The taxi stayed parallel, Lyons firing from the window, the Konzak flashing semiauto flame. The driver's window of the Dodge exploded, the spray of steel balls and glass cubes ripping away the head of the driver and killing the other gunman in the front seat. Lyons fired again, and blood and glass sprayed out the opposite window as the Dodge hurtled on toward the pickup.

"*¡Dispacio! ¡Alto!*" Gadgets called out to his driver as the Dodge crashed into the pickup. Lyons's taxi fishtailed and spun, tires smoking, rear end downing a light pole. Then Gadgets saw Lyons weaving through the smashed cars, Konzak in his hands.

Gadgets's driver stopped short. The young Mexican soldier turned to him and said in perfect English, "I'll turn the truck around and be ready for the getaway!"

Throwing open the back doors, running through the acrid tire smoke, Gadgets heard pistols popping, then the Konzak boomed. He turned to see Lyons at the Mitsubishi van.

As Gadgets approached the Dodge, he saw dead

men in the front seat. Suddenly the back door flew open, and Powell and Akbar dragged out Illovich.

"Slick hijack, Wizard!" Powell raved. "You guys got your act together."

"Get my partner's radio and pistol," Gadgets told him. "Then drag the comrade back to the truck—"

Powell threw Illovich down on the asphalt. Akbar put a foot on the back of the Soviet's neck while Powell searched the old man.

Blancanales and Desmarais stumbled from the wrecked Mitsubishi. Gadgets guided the stunned and bleeding young woman away from the wreckage. As he brushed broken glass off her clothes, Gadgets spoke like a gentleman.

"Are you okay, Mademoiselle Desmarais?" Dazed, she nodded. Gadgets pointed to the waiting panel truck. "In there, in the truck, you'll be safe. Sit down and be calm, you're safe now."

The young woman staggered away to the truck.

Then Gadgets quickly briefed his partner. "That bitch works for the Soviets. Get her into the truck and watch her. Don't let her talk to Illovich. Tell Powell and Akbar."

"You positive? She talks leftist, but—"

"She ain't leftist, she's red. We'll put the questions to her when we can."

Coming up to them, Powell tossed a Beretta 93-R and the Able Team hand radio to Blancanales. Then, jerking the Soviet cultural secretary up by his arms, Powell and Akbar dragged Illovich to the panel truck and shoved him inside.

A pistol popped, then the Konzak boomed and glass fell around Gadgets and Blancanales. Crouching down, they saw a blood-spurting Soviet flop backward through a shattered window of the Mitsubishi.

Blancanales jammed the hand radio in his pocket, then checked his pistol. "My other equipment here?"

"It's all in that truck." Gadgets pointed to the panel truck and Blancanales jogged away. "And watch that phony Frenchy."

Tires screeched, engines roared. Past the smashed Dodge and Mitsubishi, Lyons and Gadgets saw two cars full of Soviet gunmen racing toward them. The three Mexicans fired submachine guns at the approaching cars. Lyons rushed to Gadgets.

"Wizard, shut up and kill somebody," Lyons said as he pulled grenades from his bandolier, yanked the pins and threw the grenades one after another.

The first grenade exploded in a deafening boom, the next two poured out smoke. Gadgets realized the method in Carl Lyons's mayhem. The first grenade, an antiterrorist stun-shock grenade, had been designed to neutralize airline hijackers without killing passengers. It produced a blinding white flash and deafening blast but no shrapnel. The Soviets would think they faced heavy weapons. And if any local people watched the firefight in their street, the explosion served notice to take cover.

Skidding, the Soviets stopped short. The wall of smoke rising from the other grenades obscured their aim. Gadgets selected two fragmentation grenades and threw hard. His throws did not make the hundred-meter distance. The round canisters bounced off the asphalt and popped short of the Soviets.

But a 40mm high-explosive grenade from Blancanales's M-203 scored. A headless Soviet gunman fell. Another Soviet, blood jetting from a hundred pinpoint wounds, staggered backward through the confusion and drifting smoke. A police car, racing to the scene, hit the Soviet, flipping him broken-backed through the air.

Switching to a left-handed grip, Gadgets braced his CAR against the side of the wrecked Mitsubishi and aimed semiauto slugs into the corrupt Mexicans rushing to help their Soviet paymasters. Gadgets fired five rounds, dropped three gunmen, Soviet and Mexican.

Shouldering his M-16/M-203 over-and-under assault rifle and grenade launcher, Blancanales sighted down. He fired a high-explosive round under the nearest police car.

A ball of flame rushed into the sky. Lyons threw another smoke grenade. Gadgets hit two more gunmen, then flipped on his short assault rifle's safety. He added a red-smoke grenade to flames and white smoke, then watched for targets.

Firing broke out behind them. Though the rescue and quick firefight had taken only four minutes, the Soviets had already organized a response.

Lyons had anticipated the reaction. On the intersecting boulevard, Captain Soto's antiterrorist unit ambushed the cars of Soviets and corrupt Mexican police.

"Quit it, Wizard!" Lyons shouted out. "Pol! Mr. Marine! Time to go—"

Through the smoke and flames, Gadgets saw two more cars of Soviets and police rushing into the firefight. Gunmen dashed from doorway to doorway. Gadgets fired single shots from his CAR, forcing the gunmen to halt.

"Ironman! The time has come to evacuate!"

While his two buddies covered him with their submachine guns, one of the Mexican soldiers backed the pickup from the wreckage. Lyons saw the pickup coming and shouted out to Gadgets, "Wizard! Get in that truck—that one! We'll be the firepower."

"The man's got the plan!" Gadgets sprinted to the pickup and jumped in with the Mexicans. They gave him a thumbs-up congratulations on the ambush.

Gadgets saw the taxi and the panel truck starting away. Blancanales stood on the panel truck's bumper. Holding on to one of the back doors, he fired bursts of autofire from his M-16/M-203 at the Soviets and Mexican police rushing past the flaming cars.

Lyons tossed a grenade under the wrecked Dodge and ran for the pickup. As the tires squealed, the Mexicans grabbed his hands and pulled him in.

Behind them, the grenade blasted open the gas tank of the Dodge. But the spilling gasoline did not flash.

Soviets and Mexicans rushed the wrecked cars. Taking cover behind the cars, they fired at retreating Americans. An impact punched the Kevlar protecting Gadgets's chest. The Mexican next to him grunted and fell. Glass shattered. Bullets slammed the fenders.

Blancanales aimed another 40mm grenade at the gunmen. The high-explosive shell popped against the Dodge, and an explosive wave of flame enveloped the Dodge, the Mitsubishi and several gunmen.

Lyons scrambled across the pickup cargo bed to Gadgets. "You hit?"

"Where?"

"You got the bullet, you tell me."

"I'm okay, check him." Gadgets pointed to the bleeding Mexican.

A 9mm slug had passed through the upper-right section of the young man's chest and out through his back. He screamed and gasped as Lyons turned him to glance at the exit wound. Lyons saw no blood in the Mexican's mouth. He pushed him to the side of the cargo bed, out of the way of the others. "You'll live."

The pickup hurtled into another firefight. Lyons had anticipated the Soviets and Mexican-police units coming to the aid of Illovich. He had asked Captain Soto to organize an ambush. The Mexican antiterrorist officer had directed his men to take positions on the boulevard behind the scene of the rescue and wait.

When the Soviet and Mexican-police gunmen rushed to the rescue of Illovich, they ran into the trap. Firing from the cover of doorways or protected by trucks and cars and taxi cabs, the antiterrorist unit slammed the Soviets with fire from NATO-caliber FN FAL rifles, the heavy 7.62mm slugs punching through sheet steel and flesh.

All of the Soviet cars took hits, drivers and gunmen dying. But the Mexicans hesitated to fire on the squad cars. Two police cars broke through the ambush. One continued straight on down the boulevard, accelerating away at one hundred twenty kilometers an hour to safety. The other squad car stopped and returned the fire.

In the furious exchange of fire, the Soviet survivors organized a breakout.

At that moment the pickup carrying Lyons and

Gadgets and the Mexican soldiers raced into the intersection, directly into the line of fire between the Mexican ambush unit and the Soviets. The driver attempted to steer around a Soviet car, but the rear end slide slipped, and the pickup slammed broadside into an abandoned car.

Gadgets went airborne. Lyons slammed into the side wall of the pickup and bounced back. He saw his partner rolling across the asphalt. The driver floored the accelerator, and the truck spun its tires, rubber smoke clouding around Lyons as he jumped from the back of the truck.

The abandoned car separated Lyons from Gadgets. Sprinting through the smoke, slugs zipped past Lyons as the Soviets tried to kill him. He threw himself to the asphalt and crabbed around the car, autofire banging the fenders and door panels. Glass showered him.

Gadgets sat against the car, blood streaming down his face, his eyes fluttering with shock. His CAR-15 lay on the asphalt near him. Lyons snatched up the weapon and slung the CAR around his partner's neck.

"Hey, Wizard, up!"

"Man, my head...."

"Don't give me any excuses. We got work to do."

The panel truck and the other car skidded through the intersection as Lyons urged Gadgets up, Blancanales and Powell spraying fire from the back doors. Tires squealed in protest as the drivers managed very tight right turns and accelerated away.

Pulling a grenade from Gadgets's bandolier, Lyons pulled pins and threw one after another—

smoke, fragmentation, shock-stun. Then Lyons threw the last grenade from his own bandolier.

The flurry of popping grenades silenced the Soviet gunmen for a moment, and Lyons dragged Gadgets away, staggering like two drunks. The car and billowing smoke behind them provided a shield. They lurched for the safety of the far curb.

A Mexican commando broke cover. With grenades in each hand, he sprinted to the car and threw the grenades into the smoke. He pulled two more from his pockets and threw them as the others exploded. Hurrying back, he grabbed Gadgets's elbow. Running through autofire, Lyons and the Mexican carried Gadgets to the shelter of a doorway.

Bullets chipped the stone walls above them and ricochets whined into the distance as Lyons looked for Soto. A soldier with a medical kit tried to strip off Gadgets's weapons and gear, but Lyons pushed away the soldier's hands. "Forget it! Where's Captain Soto?"

"There. The Captain is there," said the man, pointing down the boulevard. "But your man is bleeding. We must help—"

"Let him bleed! We got to get out of here!" Lyons growled.

"Thanks a lot, Ironman," Gadgets said as he struggled to his feet. He leaned close to Lyons's face and blew blood off his lip, spraying a red mist into Lyons's face. "I like you, too!"

"Shut up and move—that car! Get in there."

A ricochet slashed Lyons's right shoulder and continued into the armhole of his Kevlar battle armor. His face contorting, he arched back with agony as the jagged metal slashed across his spine.

Gadgets reached out and steadied his friend. He forced a laugh. "Ironman gets his. Time to retreat."

Lyons twisted away from Gadgets's hands. "I didn't get shit! Shoot me nine zip all day long. Get in that car. In the car! Move! Move! Move!" Lyons raged, shoving Gadgets into the car. He pulled Mexican commandos from their cover and pointed to their cars.

"But American," one soldier protested. "The Russians, they come—"

A bandolier of FN FAL magazines and grenades crossed the Mexican's T-shirt. Lyons jerked a smoke grenade from the bandolier.

"I'm covering, go!" Lyons turned and threw the smoke grenade into the noise of Soviet submachine guns. He rushed along the sidewalk. "Soto! Everyone out. We got our people. Go! The Soviets don't matter now."

Soto shouted to his men. Young soldiers dodged from cover, working closer to their cars as the Soviets continued firing.

Grabbing grenades from a soldier, Lyons threw another canister of smoke at the Soviets. Then Lyons ran through the chaos with another grenade in his hand, his Konzak hanging from his shoulder by its sling as he searched for wounded. Soto shouted out.

"American! We go, we are ready!"

"No one missing?"

"All are here—"

As Lyons ran for the cars, a burst of fire whined off the stones. He felt a slug stop in his Kevlar. Spinning, his right arm cranking back with the grenade, Lyons faced a Soviet with an Uzi.

The heavy canister of explosive and steel slammed into the Soviet's chest, staggering him back. The Soviet reached for his Uzi.

Lyons had not pulled the pin of the grenade.

Crossing the distance in three running strides, Lyons kicked away the Uzi, then dropped down and smashed the Soviet in the face with the butt of his Konzak. He hammered the struggling gunman to death.

Rifles fired. Lyons looked up, saw a Soviet flipping back.

"American!" Soto shouted.

Blood and flesh covered the Konzak. He sprayed a 7-blast burst of full-auto 12-gauge, then jerked out the empty mag and reloaded on the run back to the waiting cars.

Lyons stopped with one foot in the car, the blood-slick Konzak pistol grip in his hand as his eyes scanned the street.

Nothing moved. He heard only his blood hammering in his ears. He flipped up the safety of his assault shotgun and fell into a seat as the driver accelerated away.

Sirens screamed.

16

"You cannot torture a Soviet diplomat."

"Why not?" Lyons asked.

Captain Soto watched as Blancanales poured rubbing alcohol over the blond North American's wounds. The alcohol splashed over the gouge in his shoulder and the long gash across his back. Then the medic wiped away the clotted gore. Soto watched for any change in the man's expression.

He saw the North American's eyes squint, his nostrils flare. Did he feel the searing pain?

"Why not? Tell you what. After we get the information we need, the dead meat gets disappeared."

"He is a diplomat, my friend."

"Politics?"

"International law. The customs of my country."

They sat in the office of an auto-repair garage. After the rescue and firefight, the North Americans of Able Team and the captain's disguised soldiers dispersed to avoid the police responding to the alarm. The carloads of fighters then assembled at this garage, a complex of offices, workshops and parking lots.

No one feared the curiosity of mechanics or customers. The facility served only the Condor Division, the elite battalion of the Mexican army dedicated to the extermination of foreign terrorism and the drug trade.

In Mexico, drugs and terrorism represented two faces of the same threat. Terrorists financed activities in Central and South America by the sales of drugs to the United States. Drug gangsters—dope warlords and Castillian bankers—ran the drugs north through Mexico, then smuggled weapons and dollars south through Mexico.

When an assignment required unmarked or special-purpose vehicles, mechanics provided the cars or trucks to the battalion units. The mechanics also performed the most detailed searches of seized vehicles. Though the employees worked in what appeared to be a commercial auto garage, the workers received checks from the Republic of Mexico.

This morning, after meeting Able Team at the international airport, Captain Soto gave the mechanics an afternoon's holiday. He knew the methods of Able Team. He knew his unit would see action.

Lyons considered his words, then spoke as Blancanales bandaged his wounds. "Captain, you're talking about a senior officer in the KGB. He is a cold killer. He thought nothing of joking with my friends as he took them to their execution. He's made a career of execution and torture. You heard the transmissions from that mansion. They tortured that Iranian until he broke. Then they probably put him in a hole and covered it up. We're not talking about a human being. We're talking about a torturing, murdering Soviet monster. There will be no political problems created. He will simply cease to exist when we learn—''

"And you, American? You would torture him? Then murder him? In the street a few minutes ago, in combat, I saw you as a soldier. You fought, you risked your life for your friend., then you risked your life for my soldiers. You would not escape without searching for wounded or men left behind. I respect you. But now you would torture and murder? If you did not say it yourself, if I did not watch you say the words, I would not believe it."

"Illovich is a Soviet. An officer of the KGB—"

"And in El Salvador, the death squads say 'Soviet' and they murder teachers and doctors and campesinos."

"Yeah, but we know, we're positive, absolutely—"

Blancanales cut Lyons off. "The captain won't allow it. This is, in fact, his operation. It became his operation when we entered Mexico."

"Yeah, yeah, all right...." Lyons thought about the problem for a moment. "How about if I kind of terrorize him? Don't actually touch him?"

"How?" Soto asked.

"I've got my ways. And then later on, we let him go?"

Again, Blancanales stopped the argument. "Illovich is a professional. Do you believe, even if you tortured him, he would break? I believe, that if we approach him correctly, he may cooperate."

"You're kidding! Why do you think so?"

"Understand. He had a plan worked out. His men would destroy the Iranian gang that wants to kill our President. To cover up the Soviet Union's role in the action, he intended to leave our bodies there. The bodies of two dead Americans and a Lebanese—all past or present employees of the United States government. If we take his explanation of 'world peace' seriously, he would therefore accomplish his objective without seeming to involve the Soviet Union in the problems of the United States and Iran. I can understand that.''

Lyons nodded. Pulling on a clean shirt over his bandages, he called into the garage. ''Hey! Mr. Marine! Come here.''

''What do you want, crazyman?''

''Just come here, will you?'' Lyons turned to Blancanales. ''He heard Illovich give that speech. We'll get his opinion on a straight-out request for continuing cooperation.''

The Texan bebopped into the office, snapping his fingers to a beat only he heard, singing the words, ''Kill, kill, kill. Make the world safe. Kill, kill, kill—''

''Cut it out,'' Lyons told him.

''So what's the plot?'' Powell asked. He swung his hand to slap Lyons's back. ''How you feeling, tough guy?''

Reflexively, Lyons's left hand flicked out and hit Powell's arm precisely above the elbow, on the inside where the nerves and tendons controlling hand motor function passed through the joint. The flick stopped the slap before it touched his wound.

''Excellent block!'' Powell grinned. ''Shotokan?''

''Shotokan street style. What's going on with Frenchy? She staying away from the Russian?''

''Crowd of *vatos* trying to romance her. She's still shaking from the cowboy movie. And don't worry about Illovich hearing you all. The Wizard's got headphones on Illovich, blasting him with Mexican radio. Old man's rocking 'n' rolling, shaking his bones."

"Everyone in Texas talk like you?"

"The Wizard from Texas?"

Blancanales interrupted the banter. "When Illovich delivered his world-peace speech, you think he was sincere?"

"I don't know. I know I got some peace for him. Peace by .45 Colt automatic pistol."

"That will not happen," Blancanales stated. "You think he would help us get those Iranians?"

"Maybe if you say, 'Please.' And then put a flare up his ass—"

Lyons laughed. "A rifle flare or a highway flare?"

"A rifle flare would kill him too quick. And it would most definitely get my rifle dirty."

"What we will do," Blancanales spoke over their laughter, then lowered his voice, "is offer him his life if he helps us preserve world peace."

Powell snapped his fingers. "Kill, kill, kill! Those wacky E-raquis, they got it right! Hit those E-ranies with insecticide!"

"Get serious!" Lyons faked a punch for Powell's solar plexus.

Hands flashed, the Marine officer enfolding Lyons's arm in a graceful aikaido block. Powell applied pressure to the nerves in Lyons's wrist, then released him.

"If you gentlemen are done," Blancanales said, "we can go speak to Illovich."

"You do the talking, Pol," Lyons said.

"I'll bring him in here," Blancanales continued as he looked first to Lyons, then Powell. "We are agreed? We attempt to persuade him without violence or threats?''

"Oh, sure. We'll treat him as if he were a human being.''

Powell nodded.

Blancanales left the office. As he walked through the garage, they heard him speaking to the young soldiers, joking with them, congratulating them on their fighting. Powell asked Lyons, "How come he jives with them and shuts us down?''

"They're teenagers. We're adults.''

"So we can't have a good time?''

"I've got to match you up with the Wizard. You two could do a jive duet.''

"No one can keep up with me. I'm a jive artist. I'm a master of jive. Ask Akbar. I taught him to talk. He came back from California speaking as though he were a professor of English. I set him straight.''

"Oh, yeah, no doubt. . . .''

Lyons cut his reply short as Blancanales led Illovich into the office and eased him into a straight-back chair. The Russian wore a blindfold, and his hands were bound with rope.

The blood of his driver and guard had hardened to black clots on the cultural secretary's gray suit. Bits of tape covered small cuts on his face. His head turned slowly, as if he studied the men around him through the cloth of the blindfold. No one moved, no one spoke but Blancanales.

"You said you wanted to stop the Iranian terrorists from attacking our President. Was that in fact your intention?''

"You are the Latin one?" Illovich asked. "Are you of Mexican descent? Perhaps Spanish?"

"We want the information on the Iranians."

"And if I refuse to give you that information? Do you . . . interrogate me?"

"You talked of preserving world order. If we do not have the information on the Iranians, then there is a chance we may not succeed in our mission to stop the terrorists. If they succeed in killing or even attacking our President, I'm sure there will be—"

"I understand. You are presenting my own explanation. Very well. The cause of world peace will be served."

"Where did you intend to take us?"

"They will be gone. But the man that we questioned was an officer. He knew of the next link in the organization. I suggest your force immediately goes to that place."

"Where is that?"

"A village in the northern deserts. A village named El Tecolote, on the highway north of Matehuala."

Blancanales looked to Captain Soto. Soto made the motions of dialing a telephone and started out. But Blancanales motioned him to wait.

"And what is at that village?"

"The Iranian did not know. He knew only that he would transport his units north to that village."

"And you realize, Illovich, you will accompany us to the village."

"I know."

"It will be good if you are lying to—"

"You Americans! Can't you believe that it is not in

the interest of the Soviet Union for your President to die?"

Lyons silently shook his head. Blancanales disregarded the disbelief of his partner. "We'll have to trust you. Take him back to the truck."

After Powell led the Soviet away, Blancanales asked, "Now what about the woman?"

"If we're taking Illovich, then why not her?" Lyons responded. "I say we watch her, wait for her to do something interesting. Then we jump on her."

"She conspired with Illovich," Captain Soto added, "to kill you and the others. And make it appear as if you died in an attack on the terrorists."

"Powell thinks she's got some kind of inside info on them," Lyons continued. "She's been to Syria, she's been into the Bekaa Valley. Powell said she's got a snapshot, and he wants the story on it. She keeps saying he'll get the info when they close in on the crazies. But this changes it. Maybe she doesn't have information. Maybe she's in on it. That's what I want to know. We take her with us, maybe we'll see."

"When she talked with Illovich," Soto countered, "she said nothing about the Iranians."

"Doesn't mean anything," Lyons continued his argument. "Terrorism is completely insane. She could be working for the Soviets and the Iranians. She could be working against both of them and for someone we don't even suspect. We leave her, we'll never know. We take her, maybe we'll see."

"Can we do that?" Blancanales asked Soto. "Does the woman create any problems for you?"

Soto laughed. "Much less problems than you do. Now I go. I will speak with my superiors."

Minutes later, as the Americans and Mexicans assembled their gear for the long drive, Captain Soto returned. He spread out a map on the desk in the office.

"Here is El Tecolote. Here is Matehuala. This highway comes from Mexico City and continues to the border."

"How long until we get there?" Lyons asked.

"Only a few hours—"

"No way!" Gadgets interrupted. "That looks like a day or two's cruise."

"We will take helicopters to Matehuala. They will have trucks for us there."

"Great!" Lyons told him. "Helicopters and trucks. Quite an operation, for only a few minutes' notice."

"We will be joining an operation already in progress. Last night a transport plane appeared on the coastal radar. It did not respond to requests for identification. It did not land at an airport. It continued inland and disappeared. We will join the forces searching for that plane."

17

Dust erupted into dense clouds as the four helicopters descended to the soccer field. Lyons slid open the door of the command Huey and the dust and chill December air swirled into the crowded interior, carrying away the stink of kerosene, sweat and tobacco. He shoved his shipping trunk of equipment to the edge. Though the flight north had taken only three hours, traffic and fueling delays in Mexico City had delayed the takeoff. Now Lyons wanted to move.

Parked trucks lined the soccer field, their headlights serving as landing lights for the helicopters. Drivers sat on the bumpers, waiting for the soldiers and the North American "specialists."

The skids touched the field of red dirt and Lyons jumped out, jerked out his shipping trunk after him. Three forms appeared against the headlights, the silhouettes shifting and leaping as they approached the helicopters.

Soldiers shouted to one another as they assembled in squads. Akbar led the bound and blindfolded Illovich from one helicopter. The Soviet also had rags taped over his ears to prevent his overhearing the talk around him. Blancanales, Powell and Anne Desmarais left another helicopter.

Captain Soto rushed to the three silhouettes. He

saluted. After a moment he called out to Lyons. "North American!"

Carrying his weapon-heavy trunk, Lyons lurched across the field to Soto. He saw two Mexican officers in uniform, a third man in slacks and a sports coat. The plainclothesman had an Uzi hanging over his shoulder. They shook hands with Lyons as Soto quickly introduced the officers. Soto avoided names.

"This is my commander. This officer commands this task force. This gentleman works with the *federales*." Soto used the phrase *mi amigo norteamericano* to introduce Lyons.

The Mexicans talked in rapid Spanish. Lyons stood grinning and nodding, understanding nothing. Finally Soto turned to him again. "They know of you because of General Mendez and the International. We all owe you our gratitude for breaking that gang of Fascists."

"We didn't break it. We made it bleed, but the International's still strong. It's still out there."

"But in Mexico, it is now disorganized. The drug gangs have no leadership. They are only gangs now, not an army."

"Until the International comes back. The heroin trade makes billions a month. That's too good to lose."

"We will try to stop that. My commander wants to offer to return a favor. When we fought with the International in the skyscraper of Trans-Americas, S.A., I asked you to leave and you left, leaving the glory and rewards to us—"

"You said you went to prison for a while."

"Only for a short time. It was only a political

problem. Then I received a promotion. My commander received many awards from the president of the republic because of the capture of General Mendez. Now, he offers the Iranians to you."

"Oh, yeah? You got them?"

"We know where they are. My commander offers you the opportunity to make the arrests."

Lyons shook his head. "Won't happen. There won't be any arrests. Ones we don't kill go north for interrogation. Won't ever make the newspapers."

After Soto translated Lyons's response, the three officers shook hands with Lyons and left. Confused, Lyons turned to Soto. "What's going on?" he asked.

"Now we go get them. We have until morning."

"That simple?"

"Mexican forces will move in at dawn. We must be gone by then."

Lyons ran to his partners. "Things have changed!" He explained the gift of the Iranians. After he told the story, Powell laughed.

"These Mexicans are slick! Why lose soldiers when they can have gringos get killed? And here you are jumping and laughing about it, thinking they did you such a good deed."

"Whatever. This means we dump Illovich—"

"No, this means. . . ." Powell paused, looking at the others. "We let the Russian and the Frenchy escape together. How's that? Put your microphones on them. We leave them while we go play bang bang with the E-ranies, they get away. Good enough?"

"Thought you wanted information from her?" Lyons asked.

Powell held up a black-and-white photo of two

men. "She doped herself out for the flight. So I searched her stuff and I got this. One's the Iranian we're chasing. The other one's a Syrian army officer. This is good enough. I think she's jiving me on all the other noise."

Lyons ended the conference. "That's it. No more talk. Time to do it."

A MEXICAN SOLDIER drove a stake-side truck north through the desert. After a few kilometers, he turned onto a dirt road. He switched off the headlights and drove by the moonlight, the dust and rocks of the road luminous.

Hills appeared. The driver followed the road for several kilometers, then turned into the sand and brush of a riverbed. Flash floods had cut a wide spillway through the desert. Brush and grasses grew in the sand. Following the winding stream into the hills, the driver powered over the brush, the truck's double back tires assuring traction in the sand and gravel.

After another kilometer, the riverbed became a streambed walled by high banks of sand. The driver continued through moist darkness fragrant with mesquite.

In the back of the bumping, swaying truck, Able Team changed into their fatigues. Gadgets and Blancanales wore their camou-patterned uniforms, Lyons his faded black fatigues. Powell and Akbar wore borrowed Mexican army fatigues. Captain Soto and a squad of his men would accompany them to the attack on the Iranian airstrip.

"How will he escape?" Captain Soto asked, pointing to the bound and gagged Illovich.

Lyons leaned close to the Mexican to whisper. "We will take the woman on the walk. Sometime, she'll get away from us. On the walk into the strip or during the fight. She'll come back and free him." Lyons indicated the cab of the truck with a nod. "She's up there with the driver. She knows how to get back to the highway."

"An old man and a woman? In this desert?"

"It'll be a four- or five-hour hike. They'll be back to the highway before light. If you don't like that, we could shoot them and bury them out here."

"No, let them walk."

"It's the only thing we could think of. They have to believe they escaped." Lyons stepped across the lurching deck of the stakebed to Gadgets. He glanced toward Illovich. "You got him set up?"

"Oh, yeah. That's the easy part."

"What do you mean?"

"Maybe she won't be able to find the truck. Maybe she—"

"Maybe anything. We'll see what happens."

The truck bumped to a stop. Jumping down to the sand, Lyons saw that they had come to a small waterfall. He heard the stream trickling down the face of the head-high wall of rock.

Gadgets took a case of electronic gear—the minimike receiver, an autoreverse cassette tape recorder—into the brush. There, the hidden receiver would monitor and record Desmarais and Illovich until they walked out of range.

The others assembled for the cross-country march to the airstrip. Soldiers applied face blacking and adjusted their web gear. No one smoked. No one talked. Then the voice of Desmarais broke the quiet.

"You stole it, American! I looked everywhere and I cannot find the notebook—and the photos. I know. Do not lie. I would not tell you so you stole what you wanted."

"Me? Maybe you lost your notebook."

Lyons rushed to them and hissed, "Shut up!"

"He stole my photos. I would not—"

The slap sounded like a shot. Desmarais fell into the sand. Lyons crouched over her and muttered, "You keep your mouth shut. You're only here because of him, you understand? He says the word, and you stay here with Illovich."

"The Russian is here?" Now she whispered. "Why is he here?"

Lyons laughed quietly. "We've got plans for him."

"What are you talking about?"

"Hey, reporter. You're here with him—" Lyons pointed to Powell. "I don't tell you anything. Now shut up and hike. Keep up this shit and we'll work you into the plans."

As Lyons left Desmarais, Blancanales approached Lyons. He asked in a deliberately loud voice, "What about sentries?"

"Forget it. We need every man when we hit the Iranians."

"No sentries?" Blancanales repeated for the Canadian to hear. "No one to watch the truck?"

"You worried about a coyote eating Illovich? Who cares?"

The driver of the truck would be their guide to the airstrip. Born in the area, he had worked on the *ranchos* as a cowboy until enlisting in the army. He spoke no English. With a penlight, he indicated their route into the foothills on a map.

The streambed continued several kilometers through the hills to the ranch taken over by the Iranians. The ex-cowboy pointed to a road that ran north of the ranch. The army waited there. Able Team and the group of soldiers would infiltrate from the south. Any Iranians who escaped their attack would be captured by the army.

Lyons noted a bend in the stream. The topographical whorls indicated a low hill paralleling the airstrip. His finger traced the ridgeline for his partners. "That is a great position for the M-60. Could sweep the strip, the buildings, anything that moved."

Blancanales nodded. He pointed to where the streambed met the ranch. "But we'll need a blocking force here. That will drive them into the army. Does that make sense to you, Captain? Fire from the ridge, then a blocking force?"

"We'll panic them," Lyons added. "Kill all we can, then maybe they'll break and run into your soldiers."

"My commander told me," Soto emphasized, "that the terrorists are prepared to go north. Their trucks are ready. He told me not to expect a fighting force, but instead for you North Americans to take the prisoners you want, the leaders, then to drive all the other terrorists into his line. That will satisfy both our governments."

Lyons laughed softly. "He doesn't think there'll be a fight? I am not making that assumption."

The line of soldiers moved into the moonlit darkness. Led by the ex-cowboy, they zigzagged up the stone face to the next level. The streambed stretched before them, as wide as a street. Desmarais stumbled every few steps. But the others walked quietly, the only sound the squeaking of their boots in the sand.

After a half hour of fast walking, they came to the intersecting ridge. Captain Soto signaled for a rest. Lyons took the captain aside. "Here's where we split. Your man with the M-60 comes with us. I'll carry his ammo. Give him a walkie-talkie. And the woman—" Lyons glanced around. Desmarais sat at the other end of the line. "Don't watch her."

"I know."

"See you later."

Lyons walked back to Powell and Akbar, who were both checking their FN FAL rifles. Lyons motioned them forward. Blancanales led the group up the hill. Following the Mexican soldier who carried the M-60 machine gun, Lyons went last. He carried five hundred rounds of 7.62 NATO.

In the moonlight, Blancanales found a cattle path and followed it, moving quickly uphill. One hundred meters short of the crest, he cut parallel, staying below the ridgeline. At the end of the line, Lyons sweated to maintain the pace.

At a fold in the hillside, Blancanales stopped. He waited for the others to close up the line, then motioned for them to wait. He went alone to the ridge-line.

Lyons found a space between two bushes and squatted, concealed in shadows. He scanned the moonlit hillsides for movement, but saw nothing. The curve of the hillsides blocked his view of the streambed.

His hand radio clicked. Blancanales reported to his partners, "No one up here."

"What do you see down there?" Lyons asked.

"An airstrip. Looks like a cargo plane. And trucks."

"Be there quick," Gadgets told him.

The line moved uphill. Sand and loose stone slowed the machine gunner and Lyons, and they reached the top minutes after the others.

"Hey, Ironman," Gadgets taunted. "Getting old? I know you're getting slow."

Ignoring his partner, Lyons studied the ranch and airstrip below the hill. He heard the continuous popping of a generator motor providing power to the electric lights illuminating areas around several old buildings. The buildings had been the house and barn and equipment sheds of a ranch. Plastic tarps replaced the collapsed roofs.

A recently improved road led to the ranch. Two hundred meters below Lyons, a long stretch of flatland had been scraped bare of brush and rocks. A four-engine prop plane—painted black, devoid of markings—sat on the airstrip. Men moved between the cargo plane and three tractor-trailer trucks. Other men ran hoses from a gasoline truck to the wing tanks of the plane. Off to one side stood a Soviet-made multiple rocket launcher. Lyons could see the dark outline of the steel rack that housed the rockets mounted on the flatbed of the truck. The rack was angled at forty-five degrees, ready for firing. The Ironman shrugged. Maybe the rig was for defence, or perhaps the enemy was planning a few test firings; either way, the launcher had to go.

Lyons hissed to the Mexican machine gunner and pointed at the gas truck. In the moonlight, the young man's smile glowed as he extended the bipod legs of the M-60. Lyons moved over and positioned himself to feed belts of ammunition to the weapon.

Distant autofire came in a long tearing blast, and Lyons looked toward the streambed. He saw nothing. Scrambling along the ridge, he heard Blancanales calling the Mexicans.

"Captain Soto! Captain!" Blancanales whispered urgently into the Mexican army walkie-talkie.

An answer came. Autofire continued, the hammering almost overwhelming Soto's desperate voice.

"Ambush!"

18

As Blancanales jerked back the cocking handle of the machine gun, Lyons crabbed across the ridge to his partner's position.

"Wait!" Lyons rasped. "Hold it. Don't hit them down there. Don't."

"What are you thinking?" Blancanales asked.

"If we hit them," Lyons said as he glanced to the airstrip and rancho, "they know we're up here. Give me five minutes. I'll try to come up behind that ambush. If Soto or any of his soldiers are alive, or if they're captured, I can get them out. Then you hit the Iranians."

"Can you get down there?"

"Yeah, I can. It's downhill. Five minutes?"

"Go. We'll wait."

Sliding, running, side slipping with every step, Lyons cut across the hillside. He made no effort at silence for the first three hundred meters. The continuous firing of the Iranians and Mexicans continued. He ran through the moonlight, zigzagging through the brush, sprinting the open stretches.

As he ran, he cursed his acceptance of official Mexican liaison. He did not know, but he suspected—he believed—the Mexicans had betrayed them. Captain Soto's battalion commander had sketched the path of approach to the rancho. Lyons remembered Captain Soto talking of his commander's assurances that the Iranians would scatter in the assault.

And then Captain Soto had walked into an ambush.

The autofire sputtered out to isolated bursts and shots. Lyons heard men shouting to one another in the darkness. They did not shout in Spanish.

Lyons slowed to a silent walk as he rounded the curve of the hill. He crouched down and scanned the hillsides and gully. He saw the streambed, the brush and small trees black in the moonlight. Flashlights appeared. Lyons stayed low in the sage, his black gear and faded black fatigues like a shadow on the hillside. He crept to the drop-off.

Below him, he heard the sound of footsteps in the streambed and saw Desmarais running through the sand and grasses. She looked back, fell, then ran again.

A submachine gun fired upstream. Slugs tore through the brush, snapping twigs and branches, the bullets continuing into the distance. A hand waved a flashlight over the brush. Rifles boomed and the flashlight spun back through the air, a man crashing back and moaning. Men shouted. Others thrashed through the scrub.

Desmarais continued downstream. Lyons unslung his Konzak. He thought of killing the Canadian, the thought making him grin. She deserved it, but the woman had a role to play. Instead, Lyons moved upstream.

Ahead he heard men moving through the brush. Boots ground pebbles, broke dry leaves. Weapons clinked. Lyons squatted and watched.

Dark shapes moved against the night sky. A head turned. He saw moonlight gleam on the sweat-slicked features of a Mexican. The Mexican motioned. Three men rushed out, two of the Mexican soldiers on each side of a third, supporting the wounded man as he limped along. The pointman held his position until another soldier scrambled out of the gully.

The last two Mexicans covered the others, then followed twenty steps behind. In a leapfrog retreat, one of the soldiers went low, his FN FAL rifle at his shoulder while the other continued. Then the second man stopped to cover the other. In front, the first three soldiers moved fast despite the wounded man. These five Mexicans had escaped the ambush.

Noise and voices came from the streambed. A submachine gun fired a long burst, slugs ricocheting into the sky. Silence followed.

On the hillside the five Mexicans went flat.

Men stomped through sand, weapons clattered, arms thrashed through branches. More dark forms emerged from the streambed. Lyons saw the distinctive shapes of Uzi submachine guns and Kalashnikov rifles.

The group of men advanced from the streambed. Lyons heard other voices in the streambed. He let the Konzak hang by its sling from his shoulder. Slowly, silently, Lyons worked two fragmentation grenades loose from his bandolier.

Sudden bursts of rifle fire knocked down the Iranians. The falling men sprayed aimless rounds into the night, into the brush, one Iranian shot another. Other Iranians, protected by the wall of the gully, fired at the flashing muzzles of the Mexicans' FN rifles.

Lyons pulled the pin on the first grenade and let the safety lever flip away. He counted off seconds, then lobbed the grenade on the count of four.

As the grenade exploded, thousands of wire razors slashed into the backs of the Iranians sheltered in the gully. Bodies tumbled into the streambed. Screams and sobs came from wounded.

The Mexicans threw grenades, three or four crashing into the brush concealing the Iranians. Lyons went flat on the hillside as gunmen shouted and broke cover for the gully. The explosions chopped brush and flesh with interlocking hemispheres of shrapnel.

But some of the Iranians managed to scramble back to the safety of the gully. Lyons jerked out the pin on the second grenade. The Mexicans threw another volley of grenades, but they fell short, exploding in the brush of the hillside above the gully. Autofire from the Uzis and Kalashnikovs of the Iranians answered the Mexicans.

Again counting to four after the safety lever flipped away, Lyons underhanded the second fragmentation grenade into the shadows of the gully. After the blast, Lyons heard only moans.

"¡Mexicanos! ¡No dispare! ¡Norteamericano aquí,"* he called out to the soldiers.

"Who is it?" Captain Soto's voice came back.

"It's me," Lyons said as he rushed through the brush. "Don't shoot."

A penlight blinked, and Lyons went to Captain Soto. As another soldier watched for Iranians, they had a whispered conference.

"Where are the other North Americans?"

"Up on the ridge—" Lyons looked at his watch.

Eight minutes. They should have started firing. His hand radio buzzed at that moment.

"We heard the shooting."

"We ambushed the ambushers. What do you see down below?"

"They're moving the gas truck. We can't hold off any longer."

"Then don't. Hit them."

"What about you?"

"Hit them. Let me worry about what I'll do."

"Here it goes. . . ."

NATO-caliber weapons fired on the ridgeline.

"How badly wounded is that man?" Lyons asked Soto.

"The bullet broke his ankle. You want to continue to the *rancho*? We can. He will stay—"

"Let's go."

TRACERS SPARKED off the hard-packed earth of the airstrip. Blancanales clicked up the elevation wheel on the sight of the M-60 machine gun and fired again. The burst passed over the gasoline truck. Activity around the plane stopped as the workers stared at the orange streaks.

As the Mexican machine gunner supported the belt of 7.62mm NATO cartridges, Blancanales fired a long burst into the truck, adjusting his aim as the first tracer bounced off the top curve of the gasoline tank. The next tracer disappeared into the dark form of the five-thousand-liter tank.

Then the truck disappeared in a flash of yellow light. The tracer had sparked the gasoline vapors remaining in the empty tank, the mixture of vapor and oxygen exploding. Liquid gasoline remaining in the bottom of the tank vaporized, the blast becoming a fireball rising into the night sky.

The Iranians nearest the truck died of concussion and fragmentation wounds, then the searing fireball melted their flesh. Jagged plates of steel spun in all directions, slicing through men and trucks. Steel slashed through the wings and fuselage of the cargo plane, and aviation fuel poured from the wing tanks.

Then Blancanales swept the aim of the M-60 to the plane. A tracer arched into the torn wings and the fuel flamed. Pools of fire spread around the pyre. Flaming men ran from the fires.

The truck and trailer next to the plane burned for seconds, then disintegrated in a screaming explosion of munitions, jets of white flame shooting from the yellow fires, metal spinning into the air, then only twisted steel framing remained.

Blancanales saw a figure race to the cab of the rocket launcher and climb in. He quickly pulled the big gun on line and punched tracers through the windows of the cab, chewing up metal, glass and flesh. Almost instantly, the night sky was ripped apart as the rockets in the launch rack ripple fired. Comets of flame raged through the darkness in a giant pyrotechnic display. As the Politician watched, three figures stumbled from the cloud of smoke and gases at the rear of the flatbed, their bodies clothed in flame and twisting with pain. They had been caught in the backflash. Blancanales brought the M-60 around and fired a burst of mercy kill.

Rifles on the ridge hit other targets, and flames soared into the sky, illuminating the Iranians around the trucks and buildings. Powell and Akbar fired single shots from their FN FAL rifles, knocking down standing figures, forcing others to run for cover. Gadgets popped at the Iranians with his short CAR-15.

A second diesel truck, farthest from the flaming explosion, attempted to escape from the airstrip inferno. Pulling away from the flames, the truck headed toward the ranch, then began a wide left turn. The cab bumped and swayed over mounds of dirt and brush. As the truck turned onto the road, a line of tracers from the M-60 found the cab.

The driver died instantly, but the truck lurched on, leaving the road and bumping up the hillside. Blancanales continued firing. Tires blew and the trailer lurched, and the truck ground to a stop fifty meters up the hillside.

Blancanales turned his fire on the ranch house. He saw muzzles flashing from the windows, and slugs sparked off the rocks beneath the ridgeline, the ricochets humming past. Sighting on a window, Blancanales triggered a long burst, adjusting his aim until the line of tracers entered the window. He paused as the Mexican gunner linked a second belt onto the end of the first belt of NATO cartridges.

The rifle fired again from the window. Slipping a 40mm shell into his M-16/M-203, the Politician flipped up the grenade sights and steadied the forestock on his sack of 40mm shells as he aimed at the ranch house. The grenade dropped through the plastic sheet covering the ranch house and ripped the interior with spring-steel shrapnel.

A second shell of high explosive arched into a workshop. No more rifle fire came from the buildings.

"Bang...bang...bang," Powell chanted as he squeezed off single shots. "This gang of E-ranies ain't going north. Ain't going nowhere, no way...."

Rifles flashed from every shadow and ditch below them. Slugs zipped past the ridgeline. An RPG launcher flashed, the rocket streaking past them to explode hundreds of meters in the sky.

Blancanales shouldered the M-60 again. Sighting on the shadow concealing the rocket gunner, he fired burst after burst of heavy slugs.

Another rocket shot up at them and fell short, the blast throwing up dust and debris, leaving a ten-meter-long strip of flaming brush.

"Powell!" Blancanales called out. "Over here. Take my grenade launcher. Put some high ex down there."

"Lay cool, Marine," Gadgets called out. "I'll do it. This M-zip no zap *nada* no way."

"Three points!" Powell raved. "That's no lame-loser lingo. That's high jive."

"Quit the talk!" Blancanales shouted out. "Put out rounds!"

Gadgets took the M-16/M-203 and the canvas bag of 40mm shells. He chambered a shell and snapped closed the launcher. "Where's the man with the rockets?"

"Right...there," Blancanales said as he triggered another long burst, three tracers arching down into the shadow.

A 40mm grenade followed the tracers. High-explosive popped and a rocket went wild, streaking over the roofs of the ranch buildings and hitting the hillside near the wrecked truck and trailer. Brush flamed.

Reloading quickly, Gadgets watched an Iranian run from the ranch and take cover in the gully beyond. Other Iranians followed, sprinting away from the flames and slaughter. A line of rifles fired from the embankment.

Slugs zipped past the ridgeline. Gadgets searched through the bag of grenades, squinting at the markings in the moonlight. He found what he wanted. Laughing, he chambered the shell and sent it down.

White phosphorus sprayed the gully. A man ran from the fire, points of white flame glowing on his body. He stumbled into the weeds and fell, flames and smoke rising as his body ignited the weeds.

Gadgets aimed a second white phosphorus grenade into another section of the gully. The chemical fire sprayed twenty meters of brush and weeds, flames coming immediately. An Iranian ran from the brushfire. As the Iranian stood silhouetted against the flames, Gadgets saw the M-60 and the rifles stagger him, multiple hits throwing him back into the fire.

"That Jap Jeep!" Gadgets shouted out as he slammed a 40mm shell into the grenade launcher. "Pol, hit it!"

A four-wheel-drive Toyota wove across the ranch, swerving around running men and flaming brush. Blancanales sent a line of tracers at it, missing as the Toyota wove across the airstrip then disappeared behind the flames and black smoke of the burning plane.

Blancanales estimated the Toyota's path. Arcing tracers past the plane's flames, he waited for the sight of the Toyota. Gadgets fired a high-explosive grenade. The distant pop raised a circle of dust.

The Toyota reappeared, racing in the opposite direction. Jumping ditches, swaying wildly, the Toyota accelerated on the stretch of road. Tracers and rifle fire followed it, but the zigzagging vehicle hurtled past the house, struck a running Iranian, then disappeared again, this time into the darkness at the south end of the ranch.

Powell and Akbar continued firing. Blancanales shouted, "Stop! Our partner's—"

"Damn, that E-ranie made it away!" Powell cursed.

Gadgets laughed. "Not yet...."

19

Engine screaming, the Toyota low geared through the brush and small trees. Lyons saw the driver wrench the wheel and the wagon dropped down the gully wall. The tires sprayed mud from the stream.

"Soto!" Lyons hissed.

The young infantry captain turned, the angles of his Nahuatl features silhouetted against the fires. The noises of splashing and slamming continued as the four-wheel drive vehicle maneuvered through the darkness. Soto issued quick instructions to his three remaining soldiers, then edged back to Lyons.

"That car," Lyons told him. "It could be leaders. What do you say you and me try to take them prisoner?"

Soto nodded. He crouchwalked back to the nearest Mexican soldier. On the distant ridgeline, Lyons saw the muzzles of weapons flashing, a machine gun and several rifles firing down at the ranch. No organized resistance countered the attack. Kalashnikov rifles and Uzis popped from time to time as individual Iranians blindly sprayed bullets at the hill, but their firing only attracted the downward directed aimed fire of the attackers' NATO-caliber weapons.

When Soto returned, they moved south again, retracing their path above and parallel to the gully.

They heard the Toyota crashing through brush, the engine roaring as the driver tried to double clutch. Then gears shrieked and the motor died.

Doors slammed and men cursed and shouted. Lyons moved quickly, silently, Soto a shadow a few steps back. They gained on the voices.

In the gully, flashlights lit the darkness. Lyons slowed, his steps silent in the sand of the hillside. He found a break in the weeds and brush, and going flat, he looked down into the gully.

Two Iranians were attempting to push the Toyota off a rock. The rock had bent the front bumper, then smashed into the frame. Pinned, the front wheels off the ground, the rear wheels in water and mud, the Toyota could go neither forward nor backward.

Then, in the reflecting yellow glow of a flashlight, Lyons saw the faces of the men. One had the thick features and beard of an Iranian Revolutionary Guard. But the other man had black skin and African features. His Afro shone like a halo when a flashlight swept past him.

Soto slid up beside Lyons. He noticed the black man and whispered to Lyons, "A negro?"

"Yeah." The grunting and cursing of the two men and the distant battle covered their whispered words. "Bet you a thousand pesos he's an American. A *norteamericano*. We ran into a black nationalist in Beirut," Lyons said.

"I cannot understand. Black North Americans attacking the United States?"

"They hate whites. They think whites are devils created by God. They say they are Muslims, but real

Muslims don't accept them. I guess he's working with the Iranians to kill white people."

The Iranian and the black man froze. Had they heard Lyons and Soto?

Autofire sprayed the Toyota, slugs hammering the heavy steel bumper, shattering the windshield and side windows. The two men went flat in the mud. The black man unslung an Uzi and sprayed out a magazine of 9mm.

Then both men ran. Forms splashed through the stream, muzzle-flashes from an Uzi tracking the retreating Iranian and black. But the noise of the men running—splashes and curses and arms thrashing against branches—continued to the north, back to the *rancho*.

A Mexican soldier rushed to the Toyota and looked inside. He carried an Uzi. Web gear taken from Iranians crisscrossed his camou-patterned fatigues. A second Mexican appeared, his bloody right arm strapped against his body, his FN FAL slung over his back. The wounded man held a pistol in his left hand.

"*¡Mis muchachos!*" Soto called out. "*¡Tus vivas! ¡Vienen aquí! ¡Aquí!*"

The Mexicans stared around them, startled by the voice. Captain Soto blinked his penlight, then pointed it upward to illuminate his face for his soldiers. They smiled.

As they came to the gully wall, Lyons reached down and pulled the Mexicans up. Captain Soto whispered and laughed with them. They checked the wounded man's arm. Then the two soldiers traded weapons, the wounded man taking the Uzi and the

9mm magazines, the other soldier taking the FN FAL and all the ammunition. The wounded man gave Lyons and the Mexicans a left-handed salute and hurried into the moonlit brush of the hillside.

"I sent him to wait with the other wounded man," Captain Soto explained. "Now we pursue the terrorists."

"We take them alive," Lyons stressed. "That black one could lead us into his organization up north. And the other one? Who knows?"

Soto nodded and translated to the other Mexican. They marched north again, moving fast along the now-familiar path. Ahead they heard only occasional bursts and single shots of gunfire from the *rancho*. A vast column of black smoke rose against the night sky, obscuring the stars and moon. As Lyons ran, he saw ashes falling, like black snow.

They soon overtook the two terrorists. Slinging his Konzak, Lyons pulled his silenced auto-Colt. He eased back the slide to chamber the first hollowpoint and thumbed up the ambidextrous fire selector to safe.

A rifle fired. One of the Mexican soldiers watching the *rancho* had killed a fleeing Iranian with a point-blank NATO slug to the chest.

In the gully, the other terrorists went silent. Lyons waited, listening. He heard their feet on the rocks of the streambed. A pair of boots splashed through the water. He listened as the sounds of boots on rocks, then boots breaking dry weeds crossed to the opposite side of the gully.

Lyons turned to Soto and the other soldier. "Captain, I'm going alone. Tell your men not to shoot me.

Not to shoot anyone over on that side of the stream. Might be me.''

"And what of the North Americans there?'' Captain Soto pointed to the ridge.

"Just a second. . . .'' Lyons spoke into his hand radio. "Calling Politician, calling Mr. Wizard. What goes on?''

"What you see is what we did,'' Gadgets answered. The hammering of the M-60 machine gun continued behind his voice. "Did you get the ones in that Toyota?''

A line of tracers arched down. Lyons watched an Iranian break cover and run to the shelter of a ditch. Silhouetted against the burning ranch buildings, the Iranian raised a Kalashnikov and fired at the ridge. One of the Mexican soldiers near Lyons sighted carefully and put a bullet through the Iranian's back.

"I'm chasing them. One's an Iranian, who may be a leader. The other one's a negro male. Might be a black nationalist, like we encountered in Beirut. They cut to the west. I'll be following them. Why don't you send Powell and Akbar down to talk to the Iranians. Maybe some of them will surrender.''

"That's an idea. Happy hunting.''

Lyons clipped the radio to his web belt. One step took him down the gully in a controlled slide. He paused, listening. He heard only the firing of rifles and autoweapons.

Light from the flames rising from the airstrip and ranch created shadow along the east side of the gully. Lyons stayed in the shadow, his boots silent in the soft sand. He moved quickly for a hundred meters, then slowed as he approached a curve in the stream.

Crossing the stream, he went flat and peered around the curve. Smoke from smoldering brush obscured his sight. A blackened corpse lay in the stream. He saw no one moving, heard no shooting.

He clawed up the gully wall to the hillside opposite the *rancho*. Taking his hand radio from his belt, he reported his position. "I'm on the west side of the creek, going north."

Blancanales answered. "I think I spotted them. There's a section of burning brush—"

"Yeah, I'm at the south end."

"I saw them come out of that."

"Can you slow them down without killing them?"

"Maybe. . . ."

On the ridge, the muzzle of the machine gun flashed. A line of tracers cut through the smoke. For Lyons, the tracers pinpointed the position of the terrorists. He moved quickly through the sage and small trees, the auto-Colt in his hand.

The NATO-caliber slugs hit with a sound like a whip, striking with a dull crack, followed by the sound of the bullets ripping through the air. A tracer ricocheted past Lyons, the pinwheeling bullet passing him and ripping into dry brush. Other ricochets hummed past, invisible.

Another projectile came down, this one slow, rushing through the air, then exploding fifty meters north. Bits of wire shrapnel rained around Lyons. Then he heard the black man, "Those white motherfuckers are throwing all kinds of shit down! They got to know who we are, they got us spotted, we got to—"

The Iranian interrupted in another language. Switching to that language, the black man continued as Lyons crept ahead. Finally Lyons could not risk approaching closer. The terrorists had the embankment shielding them from Blancanales's machine gun fire. Lyons did not.

He reached to the hand radio. Turning off the voice speaker, he clicked the transmit key three times, then three times again.

Talking fast, in what Lyons assumed to be Arabic, the black man scrambled for the top. He reached back to help up the Iranian. On the ridge, Blancanales fired again, tracers sparking off the rocks only three steps away from the black man. The black dropped the Iranian and ran into the flames of the *rancho*.

As the Iranian pulled himself to the top of the gully, Lyons lined up his auto-Colt's tritium dots on the right knee of the Iranian. He fired once.

The forty-five-caliber hollowpoint smashed through the cartilage and tendons and bones of the Iranian's leg. He fell screaming. Rolling on his back in the streambed, he reached for his knee. He found his leg, flopping, folded backward over his thighs. Blood spurted from the severed artery.

Lyons jumped into the sand. The Iranian saw him and reached for his pistol. Lyons fired again; the slug smashed the Iranian's hand to ragged flesh and shattered on the steel of the holstered pistol, spraying lead fragments.

Blood gushed from the mangled hand. Staring into the suppressor of the auto-Colt, the Iranian raised his hands and pleaded.

"Please...I Rouhani, leader of Revolutionary Guards. No kill, please! No!"

Lyons kicked Rouhani in the head, stunning him. As the Iranian cried and babbled in Arabic, Lyons flipped him onto his face. He used the plastic loops of riot cuffs as tourniquets on his forearm and above his gory knee. Then he linked the tourniquet on his right forearm to his left arm with another loop of space-age plastic, effectively immobilizing the maimed Iranian terrorist. Lyons spoke into his hand radio, "Got the Iranian. Claims he's a leader. You see where the black creep went?"

"Into the fires," Blancanales replied. "He's dodging over to the road, up against the foot of the hill."

"Where you can't hit him—"

"He thinks—"

"Don't. But slow him down."

Unslinging his Konzak, Lyons ran through the smoke and blackened brush of the gully. An Iranian hiding in the weeds turned. His eyes didn't register the black-uniformed, black-faced American for an instant, then he jerked up his Kalashnikov.

But far too late. Blasts of steel shot tore away his hands, destroying the AK he held, the shots continuing through his arms to scramble his guts, the second blast spraying Number Two and double O shot through his lungs and heart. Thrown back by the impact, already dead, the Iranian collapsed in a bloodied heap as Lyons continued past without breaking stride.

Leaving the gully, Lyons continued through the clouds of black smoke stinking of rubber and plastic and flesh. To his left, flames and smoke rose from the gutted hulks of the trucks and plane. To his right, the buildings of the ranch burned.

Squinting against the smoke and heat, he saw

tracers skipping off the hillside. The black terrorist dodged from cover to cover. Sometimes smoke from the burning hillside brush screened him. In front of the terrorist, the crashed truck and trailer continued to burn.

The black terrorist chanced the open ground. Lyons saw him zigzagging to cover. Sprinting diagonally across the corner of the airstrip, Lyons dived into a ditch. He laid his Konzak within reach and unholstered his auto-Colt. Flipping down the left-hand grip lever, Lyons braced the heavy pistol on the edge of the ditch and waited.

Rising from a shadow, the black man ran toward the road.

Twenty meters to his side, flame exploded from the trailer. Torn aluminum and scraps of metal tumbled across the open ground, carried along by a tremendous jet of fire.

A rocket hurtled through the opposite side of the trailer, tearing through the aluminum. Shooting out a tail of flame, the rocket spun wildly through the night and exploded. Other rockets flashed simultaneously, their launching jets coming in one wave of superheated gases and vaporized aluminum, every combustible thing near the wrecked truck and trailer suddenly burning.

The black man, who had conspired with foreign terrorists to assassinate the President of the United States, stood in an incandescent wind. Lyons saw the man's clothing flame away, then his flesh, bones suddenly visible in that instant of cremation. Lyons went flat in the ditch.

Flames and shredded metal continued streaking

into the *rancho*, burning what had not yet burned, charring the dead. Rockets flew wildly from the trailer, then the trailer exploded in a giant fireball.

Metal and flaming solid propellant fell around Lyons. When he looked up, nothing remained.

TWO DAYS LATER, in the devastated village of the Bekaa Valley, a messenger delivered a message to the desk of Colonel Dastgerdi. The Syrian officer waited until the soldier left his office, then tore open the envelope. The one-line communication read, "They defeated the puppets."

Colonel Dastgerdi carefully burned both the typed page and the envelope, then scattered the ashes.

The Americans had taken his pawn. Now he would take their President.

Mack Bolan's

ABLE TEAM

by Dick Stivers

Action writhes in the reader's own street as Able Team's Carl "Mr. Ironman" Lyons, Pol Blancanales and Gadgets Schwarz make triple trouble in blazing war. To these superspecialists, justice is as sharp as a knife. Join the guys who began it all—Dick Stivers's Able Team!

"This guy has a fertile mind and a great eye for detail. Dick Stivers is brilliant!"

—Don Pendleton

#1 Tower of Terror
#2 The Hostaged Island
#3 Texas Showdown
#4 Amazon Slaughter
#5 Cairo Countdown
#6 Warlord of Azatlan
#7 Justice by Fire
#8 Army of Devils

#9 Kill School
#10 Royal Flush
#11 Five Rings of Fire
#12 Deathbites
#13 Scorched Earth
#14 Into the Maze
#15 They Came to Kill

Able Team titles are available wherever paperbacks are sold.

GOLD EAGLE

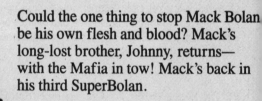

Able Team is a Winner!

What readers are saying about Able Team

"Action-packed! No other adventure series can hold a candle to Able Team. Keep up the good work!"
—*R.D., Caneyville, KY*

"Fast moving and full of action. If only they made movies like Stivers writes books!"
—*R.G., Newark, DE*

"The world needs men like Bolan and his hell-wringers, Able Team and Phoenix Force—men of justice and integrity! Your books are literary magic. I hope they stay around forever."
—*G.H., Smithers, BC*

"Able Team's fast-moving excitement makes me feel I'm right there and part of the action. I love it!"
—*V.B., Bowling Green, IN*

GOLD
EAGLE